Coming Home for Her
Life In Live Oak

Jessika Klide

This is a work of fiction. Names, characters, organizations, places, events, and incidents are either products of the author's imagination or are used fictitiously. Any resemblance to actual events, locales, or persons living or dead are entirely coincidental.

© 2023 JESSIKA KLIDE LLC ALL RIGHTS RESERVED

No part of this book may be reproduced, or stored in a retrieval system, or transmitted in any form or by any means electronic, mechanical, photocopying, recording, or otherwise, without express written permission of the publisher.

This book is licensed for your personal enjoyment only. This book may not be re-sold or given away to other people.

Published by Jessika Klide, LLC

Editing by: Maria Clark

Formatting by: Jessika Klide, LLC

Published in the United States of America

Contents

The Navy Seal Creed	vii
Prologue	xi
Chapter 1	1
Chapter 2	13
Chapter 3	23
Chapter 4	33
Chapter 5	41
Chapter 6	47
Chapter 7	57
Chapter 8	69
Chapter 9	81
Chapter 10	89
Chapter 11	97
Chapter 12	103
Chapter 13	113
Chapter 14	121
Chapter 15	127
Chapter 16	135
Chapter 17	141
Chapter 18	149
Chapter 19	155
Chapter 20	163
Chapter 21	169
Chapter 22	175
Chapter 23	183
Chapter 24	191
Chapter 25	199
Epilogue	209

Want to Read Jessika's newest, sexiest, and most talked about bestsellers?	217
Jessika Klide	219

For all the military service dog heroes.

The Navy Seal Creed

In times of war or uncertainty there is a special breed of warrior ready to answer our Nation's call. A common man with uncommon desire to succeed.

Forged by adversity, he stands alongside America's finest special operations forces to serve his country, the American people, and protect their way of life.

I am that man.

My Trident is a symbol of honor and heritage. Bestowed upon me by the heroes that have gone before, it embodies the trust of those I have sworn to protect. By wearing the Trident, I accept the responsibility of my chosen profession and way of life. It is a privilege that I must earn every day.

My loyalty to Country and Team is beyond reproach. I humbly serve as a guardian to my fellow Americans always ready to defend those who are unable to defend themselves. I do not advertise the nature of my work, nor seek recognition for my actions. I voluntarily accept the inherent hazards of my profession, placing the welfare and security of others before my own.

I serve with honor on and off the battlefield. The ability to control my emotions and my actions, regardless of circumstance, sets me apart from other men.

Uncompromising integrity is my standard. My character and honor are steadfast. My word is my bond.

We expect to lead and be led. In the absence of orders,

I will take charge, lead my teammates, and accomplish the mission. I lead by example in all situations.

I will never quit. I persevere and thrive on adversity. My Nation expects me to be physically harder and mentally stronger than my enemies. If knocked down, I will get back up, every time. I will draw on every remaining ounce of strength to protect my teammates and to accomplish our mission. I am never out of the fight.

We demand discipline. We expect innovation. The lives of my teammates and the success of our mission depend on me — my technical skill, tactical proficiency, and attention to detail. My training is never complete.

We train for war and fight to win. I stand ready to bring the full spectrum of combat power to bear in order to achieve my mission and the goals established by my country. The execution of my duties will be swift and violent when required yet guided by the very principles that I serve to defend.

Brave men have fought and died building the proud tradition and feared reputation that I am bound to uphold. In the worst of conditions, the legacy of my teammates steadies my resolve and silently guides my every deed.

I will not fail.

Prologue

The beginning of the school year.

Jorja Jones

A pair of size fourteen Converse sneakers come into view.

Oh no! Please don't let his locker be anywhere near mine!

I glance up to see a smirk on Jocko Monroe's face. He has a twinkle in his eyes as he hovers, looking down at me.

I slam my locker door, spin the lock, and stand, glaring at him. Hoping I make it crystal clear, I want no part of him or his derogatory comments.

He may be the biggest athletic stud to grace the halls of Live Oak High, but he's also the biggest prick.

He leans down from his 6'4" height to laugh in my 5'4" ear. "Sup, Juicy?"

Trying to ignore him but knowing he won't let me, I roll my eyes as I close them and grit my teeth. "It's going to be a long year if you keep calling me that!"

He chuckles, and dammit, it sounds as sexy as he is. He croons, making my knees weak. "You and I both know it's true."

I bite my tongue because he's right. The minute I catch a whiff of his musky scent, my panties are wet, and it pisses me off that I can't control the way my body reacts to him. But I'm no one special. He gets this reaction from all girls.

Jocko is too arrogant and too cocky because he's too gorgeous. However, I refuse to fawn over his perfect ass like everyone else. It's disgusting the way they prostrate themselves, wanting his attention. I have more self-respect than that and self-discipline.

Besides, he's not boyfriend material. He's mean.

Defiant, I sling my backpack over my shoulder in a pitiful attempt to knock him away.

He laughs harder, then whispers in my ear. "I like feisty."

"God, you are so infuriating! Why do you torture me?"

"Because I want to ... and because you are so damn delicious when you get all pissed off."

I raise my hand to push him away but stop myself just in time. *If my pussy soaks itself with his scent, how will it betray me if I touch his muscular body?* It drops harmlessly by my side. *I don't need to make that mistake.* "Move, Jerk-off. I'm going to be late for class."

He laughs out loud at my feisty, pissed-off comeback, enjoying my resistance way too much, but he steps back.

Without another word, I stomp off, but I can feel his eyes watching me.

At the end of the lockers, Macey giggles when I walk up. "Jocko teasing you again?"

I grit my teeth and nod my head. "It's going to be a long year. His locker is close to mine."

She giggles harder. "Honestly, Jorja, I don't know what your problem is. If Jocko Monroe were flirting with me like that, I would be in heaven!"

I roll my eyes at her. "He'a not flirting. He's being a bully! You don't know him like I do."

She snorts. "What's there to know? He is 6'4" and glorious!"

"He's an ass!"

"So?" She shrugs. "He's a 6'4" glorious ass!"

I shake my head. "Come on. We don't want to be late for class."

Jocko

Watching Jorja stomp away is nearly as good as staring down her shirt at her tits while she knelt at her locker. Her body's built to make a man moan, and her anger adds a sexy twitch to her stride that jerks her booty from side to side.

I'm going to enjoy my senior year much more than I thought.

"Hey, Jocko," Britney says as she slinks in to take Jorja's place. Her eyes are glued to me like I'm her next meal. *No, thank you.*

I spin the lock on my locker, keeping a wary eye on her. She's grabbed my junk before.

She steps closer, and I open the locker door, ignoring her. "So, is it true you throw a 100-mile-an-hour fastball?"

I press my lips together, shut my locker and give her a look that says, 'I don't have time for your stupid games.'

She knows it's true. The whole damn county knows it's true. A pro scout was down last week and clocked it.

Before that, I was just the 'big man' on campus. Which was bad enough. But now I'm some sort of 'star', and everyone wants a piece of me.

Everyone but Jorja. She's the only one unfazed.

I ignore Britney and walk off, but she follows hot on my heels, like a bitch in heat, pissing me off. I do an about-face and crush any romantic notions she has. I glare at her and spit, "Barbara, back off."

My face-to-face assault halts her, but she informs me, "My name isn't Barbara."

"Whatever your name is, then. Stop following me. You are fucking ugly."

Her face reflects the verbal slap, then she glances around to see if anyone overheard. I don't wait to watch her slink away. I turn and head to class. I glare at the pack of girls waiting in the hall. I'm disgusted with myself for not finding a better way to handle them. But honestly, the only way to back off bullies is to be a bigger one.

My mother would roll over in her grave if she knew how I spoke to them. But then again, maybe she wouldn't. No mother wants their child bullied, and it's been happening since my growth spurt. And it's really taken a significant turn to hardcore harassment since my fastball has made me famous.

The end of the school year.

Parking my jeep at Live Oak High, I head inside. It's only been a week since graduation, but I already feel out of place. Walking through the hall, the atmosphere is relaxed. Everyone's milling around, waiting for the bell to ring on the last day before the summer break.

When I round the corner to the lockers, I see Jorja. Her back is to me, and she's leaning on my old locker laughing with Macey.

I'm going to miss teasing Juicy.

Joseph Pruitt walks up to her. His smile and his posture piss me off.

He's hitting on her.

When she smiles at him, a vise clamps down on my heart.

When he hands her his phone, an unknown force punches the wind out of my gut.

When she begins to tap the device, giving him her digits, the realization of how I really feel hits me right between the eyes, and I advance on them with more forceful intensity than I originally intended this goodbye to have.

Macey's face lights up when she sees me, then her mouth drops open, and her eyes bug out of her face.

I've scared the hell out of her.

Both Jorja and Joseph turn to see what's frightened her.

My eyes lock on Joseph's, and he starts stuttering. "Jocko, I ... I thought y ... you were gone."

I grip his shoulder, and he visibly cringes, then I hand shuck his stupid ass away. "Backoff, Motherfucker." I growl.

He stumbles, slips, lands on his ass, then crawls away.

When I turn to face Jorja, Macey takes a few steps back, clearing the space between us.

Jorja's eyes narrow, and she opens her mouth to say something sassy, but her words are lost.

I'm on her. Pushing her body against the locker, I pin her there with my own.

She stiffens in resistance, and her eyes flash with anger, then defiance.

But this time, I don't taunt or tease her. This time, I cup her face and tilt her lips to take my kiss.

As I lower my mouth to hers, the defiance in her eyes fades to fear as her willing body melts into mine.

Damn. I've been a fool. I should've done this a long time ago. She's been resisting me, not because she doesn't want me, but because she does!

My lips crush hers, and a blast of sensations overwhelms me.

The sweetness of her scent. The softness of her breath. The exquisiteness of her essence fills my emptiness completely.

I press her willing body, needing to feel her curves meld into mine. Then her lips part, and her mouth opens, wanting my tongue inside her.

All the years of hunger and longing for her burst forth, and I devour her like a starving man. Every sensation shoots through me like lightning, and I can't get enough of her.

When I finally release her mouth, silence surrounds us as I stare into her eyes, burning this moment into my brain, knowing this may be the only time I hold her in my arms.

My throat tightens with the raw emotion of saying goodbye to her, making my words impossible to express.

But I want her to know how I feel, how I've always felt towards her.

Holding her face captive, I stare into her eyes, baring my soul to her.

Jorja Jones, you have always been the only one I have wanted, and when I come home ... if I make it home ... I want to come home to you.

The bell rings.

I set her free, hoping her heart will wait for my return.

Then I turn and walk away to become the man I am meant to be. Not a professional baseball player but a SEAL in the US Navy.

1

Jocko

———

"Welcome to Live Oak, Alabama." I read the sign at the city limits. "We made it, Luce. The first stop is my parent's gravesite. I need to pay my respects. I know they would be proud of the man I have become, and I want them to meet who is responsible for my safe return home."

Driving down the road, past familiar landmarks, I open up about losing them. "The days after the accident were dark. I was so angry. I would sneak into the graveyard to sleep with them under the stars."

I hit the blinker and slow down to make the turn into Live Oak Cemetery. "Did I tell you I could have played pro baseball? No? Well, I could have. My fastball my senior year was clocked at 100 miles per hour, and pro scouts were paying attention. But I decided my life needed to matter more than making people cheer. I needed to make a difference in a more meaningful way."

Parking, I pick up the bouquet of flowers meant for my mom and open the truck door.

"Come on."

―――

Turning down Dogwood Lane, I announce our next destination and ponder out loud to Luce. "We are going to swing by Juicy Jorja's house. Not to stop by, but just to see who lives there now. Did I mention our history? I was crazy about her in high school. I teased her all the time. She hated my calling her 'Juicy,' by the way. We never dated. I wasn't brave enough to ask her out. 'Cause once you're rejected, there's no going back. But I should have. I was too stupid to see the writing on the wall. She didn't flirt back because she didn't like me too, but rather because she did and didn't want to admit it." I laugh, raising my eyebrow at him. "I know that for sure because I stole a goodbye kiss, and she melted in my arms." I grin as we approach her house. "So, did she wait for me, or will she be the one that got away? And if she got away, is she happy enough to stay away?"

We cruise by her family's old house, and there she is! Getting out of a car in the driveway. Impulsively, I hit the brakes. Years of training kick in, and I crawl by to gather intel.

The first thing I notice is her body is still built to make a man moan. All woman. All curves.

Instantly, the feeling only she ever gave me conjures a rise from my cock.

The second thing I notice is her hair is shorter, shoulder-length, and cut in layers. She bounds up the steps two at a time, and all her bouncing parts send me into the stratosphere of need.

As she unlocks the front door, I smile. *She still lives here.*

Several additional interesting things catch my eye as I pass by.

There are no toys in her yard. Therefore, she isn't a mom.

A couple of small signs are in the yard. One's an advertisement for a lawn care service. Therefore, no man in her life.

The other is a warning that her house is protected by a security system. Therefore, she lives alone.

I grin at Luce and tell him. "Maybe I scared them all away when I threatened Joseph. Now wouldn't that be something?" I laugh.

A short distance down the street, I can't believe my eyes. "Well, well! Lookie here, Luce. The house next door is for rent. What do you think? Want to live next door to my girl?"

I grin in the rearview mirror, and he smiles. "Looks like we have found a place to live."

Rounding the corner off Dogwood Lane, I tell my boy, "Our next stop is Aunt Betty and Uncle John's house. Now, listen, if Pepper is still alive, go easy on the old dog."

Waah. Waah. Two short sirens pop off, and I glance in the rearview mirror to see a cop car tailing us.

"Well, shit." I pull over on the side of the road and put my window down. "Stay calm, Luce."

I lay my pistol on the dash in clear view and dutifully put my hands on the steering wheel in plain sight.

The officer walks up and sees the handgun. Immediately, he stops and puts his hand on his weapon. "You got a permit for that?"

"Yes, sir."

"License, registration, insurance, and carry permit, please." He says firmly.

"They're in the glove box," I state without moving.

The officer takes a step back, pulls his weapon, and instructs, "Reach slowly and get them out. Keep your hands where I can see them at all times."

Just then, another cop car pulls up, and Seth Monroe, my first cousin, gets out. "What the fuck, man? Are you kidding me?" He strides over with no regard for the other officer but tells him as he passes, "Louie, put your weapon away. This is my cousin, the Navy SEAL, Jocko Monroe."

Officer Louie takes another step back as I unlatch my seat belt and exit the truck, but he only lowers his weapon. He doesn't put it back in the holster.

"Welcome home, Cuz!" Seth wraps me up in a big hug, slapping me hard on the back.

"Thanks, man. It's good to be home."

Nathaniel, Seth's partner, walks around the front of their cruiser. "Well, I'll be damned." His outstretched hand clasps mine. "Welcome home, Jocko."

Now, Officer Louie puts his gun away and offers his hand. "Nice to meet you. I have heard a lot of things about you."

"Likewise. All good, I hope."

"You just getting into town?" Seth beams. "You should have told us you were coming."

"Naw, I like having the element of surprise on my side."

They laugh.

"I hope you're heading to Mom and Dad's. She'll be upset if she isn't your first stop."

"Taking my boy to meet them now."

Seth's eyes light up. "You got a boy?" He walks over to the back door and opens it, then takes a step back.

Sitting on the edge of the seat, ears forward and alert, eyes focused and drilling Officer Louie (who he smelled fear from), totally ignoring Seth (who's a big dog lover) is my german shepherd MPC K9.

"Oh ... he's a good-looking son of bitch. What's his name?" Seth says as he waits respectfully.

"Luce."

My boy cuts his eyes at me.

"Isn't that a girl's name?" Seth teases.

"He's confident in his masculinity." I chuckle. "And ... it's short for Lucifer."

They all laugh, and Nathaniel says, "That suits him!"

I snap my fingers, and Lucifer jumps down and heels.

Officer Louie takes a step back. "Is he safe?"

"For the most part." I tease him.

I reach down and ruffle Lucifer's hair. "He's my boy. He's my good boy."

Lucifer's tongue rolls out and dangles. One ear twists to the side, and I swear, he laughs.

"Pet or K9?" Nathaniel asks, eyeing him.

"Retired with distinction, so pet now. He's an MPC, multi-purpose canine." I explain. "He does it all. I'm hoping we can hire his skills out once in a while. Part-time on emergency gigs. He tracks, sniffs bombs, drugs, and he's badass at takedowns."

"Good to know." Seth says, "I'll pass that along to Chief Kent. I'm sure the community can use his skills on occasion."

"Appreciate it. He gets bored when he isn't working."

Their radios squawk as a call comes in. Nathaniel

responds as Seth sticks his hand out. "I'm sure Mom will put together a welcome home party for you. We'll catch up then."

I shake it. "You bet."

I offer my hand to Nathaniel. "Nice to see you again."

And to Officer Louie. "Nice to meet you. We done here?"

He grins. "Yeah, you're good to go."

I look down at Lucifer. "Load up."

Seth must have called Aunt Betty and given her a heads-up that I was on my way over. She and Uncle John are standing on the porch when we pull up, beaming with pride.

For the next hour, we sit on the back deck, watching the dogs play in the yard and catch up. Lucifer runs laps around and around Pepper, who is content to let him.

I share with Aunt Betty and Uncle John as much as I'm allowed to say about our missions. Which is very few actual details, but what I can share sounds really cool to civilians.

"How long is your visit?" Uncle John asks.

"I'm home for good."

"Oh, my, that makes this old woman very happy!" Aunt Betty gets up to give me another hug.

Uncle John offers, "You're welcome to stay here while you settle in."

"Thanks, but I have already booked a cottage booked at Chapel Hill, and I saw a house on the way in that's for rent. I'm going to check into it. It would be perfect."

They exchange a look. "It wouldn't happen to be on Dogwood Lane, would it?"

A lopsided grin slides sheepishly across my face. "Maybe."

"I certainly hope so." Aunt Betty smiles.

I stand. "Listen, I have taken up enough of your time today, but I wanted to make sure I stopped by on my way in."

When I push open the office door at Baker Realty, Lucifer's on a leash.

"May I help you?" The receptionist asks.

"I'm here to rent the house on Dogwood Lane."

She looks at her computer screen and informs me, "That house's listed with Marianne Reynolds. May I have your name?"

"Jocko Monroe."

She types. "Marianne will be right out to help you."

She doesn't bother hiding her curiosity and looks me up and down. That old feeling of hide your ass, you're about to be groped returns, so I take a seat on the couch while I wait.

"He's a beautiful dog. What's his name?"

"Thank you. Luce." I look down, and he leans his head over and rubs my leg affectionately.

"Normally, we don't allow animals inside."

"Good thing he isn't an animal." I grin at her.

She smirks.

Marianne walks in all smiles. "Jocko Monroe?" She offers her hand, and I stand to shake it. "Marianne Reynolds. I understand you want to see the house on Dogwood Lane?"

I shake my head. "No, ma'am. I want to *rent* the house on Dogwood Lane."

"Well, that makes my job easy. Right this way, then."

Walking over to Live Oak Trust and Loan, Lucifer and I pass the Fire Station.

"Jocko?"

Bradley Monroe walks toward me with a huge grin on his face. He wraps me up in a big hug. "Cuz, it's good to see you."

"Good to be home."

"And who do we have here?"

"Luce."

Bradley cuts his eyes at me.

"Lucifer," I laugh.

He chuckles, rubs his head, and scratches behind Luce's ears.

"He served five of the six years with me. Saved my life more than once. He's kinda special."

Bradley ruffles his neck, talking doggy goo-goo to him, but in a manly way. "He's a good boy. A real hero."

"Yes, he is." I acknowledge.

"Mom called and told me you were home. She's already planning a welcome home dinner for you."

Just then, the firehouse lights strobe and the alarm goes off.

Bradley reacts instantly, grabs my hand, and pumps it once, "Glad you're home. Can't wait to introduce you to Diane."

"Looking forward to connecting again."

He runs inside, and I look down at Lucifer. "Come on, Luce. We don't want to get run over."

When we walk into Live Oak Trust and Loan, everyone stops and stares. A man comes out of a side office and walks over with his hand outstretched, "Jocko Monroe, I presume?"

"One and the same."

"The whole town is already talking about your return. What can Live Oak Trust and Loan do for you?"

"I'd like to open an account and transfer my funds."

"I can take care of that. Right this way." He escorts me into his office.

"News travels fast," I comment on the way as people continue to stare.

He chuckles. "Marianne called."

Lucifer and I make a quick stop by Nik's Gym and sign up for a membership. Nik is a former MMA champion and a badass. Working out and grappling will keep me in shape and my hand-to-hand combat skills sharp.

An hour later, we're heading to Milner's Airfield to see Greg. After my parents passed, Aunt Betty and Uncle John took me in. Their boys were already gone, but she made sure they were always around and included me so I wasn't alone. Of course, they turned spending time with me into a competition. But I spent the most time with Greg. He was divorced and a single dad. His son Lance was about five back then.

When I pull up to Grace-Lifeline, he's standing outside, grinning from ear to ear, dressed in his flight suit with two helmets in his hand. The first words out of his mouth when I step out is, "Airborne in five?"

"Abso-fucking-lutely!" Opening the back door, Lucifer jumps out and heels instantly. "Let me grab his flight gear."

Luce springs into the bed of the truck, sniffs through the bags, bites the one holding his gear, lifts it, and brings it to me. I unzip it and pull out his jump vest, goggles, and ear protection. "Yes, you're going," I tell him, and his tail wags.

Walking back to Greg, he starts prancing, excited to be doing something more than lounging around.

"I take it he likes to fly?"

"He likes to work, and since we have been transitioning out of the military, we haven't been able to do much of anything but run. I'm looking forward to getting settled and getting us both back in shape." I bend down and strap his gear on.

Greg scratches his cheek, smirking. "Cuz, if you're out of shape ..." He eyes me up and down, then says, "Do the Monroe brothers a favor for old times' sake? Don't challenge us in front of the wives."

I laugh. "Don't poke the bear, then."

"Fair enough."

On the way to the helicopter, he asks, "You settling down in Live Oak?"

"Yeah, I have unfinished business here."

"Her name wouldn't happen to be Jorja Jones, would it?"

I grin. "It would."

2

Jorja

Grabbing my laptop satchel off the kitchen table, I take an extra second to settle the weight on my shoulder when I catch sight of Marianne's car pulling into Mr. Finkel's driveway.

Hmm, anyone in there with her? Nope, she's alone.

Hurrying out the front door, not wanting to get caught in a conversation that will make me late for work, I hear, "Good morning, Jorja."

Glancing back with a smile but not slowing down, I give her a tiny wave and pull open the car door.

She calls across the yard. "I rented the house yesterday."

I pause with one foot in and one foot out. "That's good to hear." I toss my tote in the car and nearly lose my balance.

"You are going to love him."

"That's nice to know." I plop down in the seat.

She shoos me off. "I know you're in a hurry. You can thank me later."

"Yeah, I don't want to be late." I close the door, crank the car, and as I turn to back out of the drive ... *did she say them or him?*

When I step into Donut Dilemma for my routine coffee and cake, it's buzzing with activity, and the line is longer than usual. *Good thing I came 30 minutes early.*

Waiting for my turn, I strain to hear what the hype is all about. The couple in front of me is talking about where they want to go on vacation. Their voices drown out any actual words I might be able to hear otherwise.

When it's my time to order, I step to the counter and smile at Macey. "Morning, Boo. I'll have my usual...."

Her face contorts with excitement as she bounces up and down. "Oh, my god! Jorja!"

"Cancel that. I'll have whatever you have had."

"Jorja!" She leans over the counter. "He's home. Jocko Monroe is home!"

The blood drains from my face.

Macey jumps up and down with a crazy clown grin plastered on her face. "He came in a little while ago. Jesus! Jorja! He is huge!" She spreads her arms wide. "Oh, my god! His 6'4" frame is all filled out! Gorgeous gloriousness!" She giggles, "I dropped the coffee pot. I was so shocked and..." She leans toward me and whispers, "Damn! Turned on!" She pauses, lost in her memory, visualizing his manliness. "He is ALL MAN!"

She regains her composure and shouts my order over her shoulder. "One gigantic vanilla latte and a piece of peach to go!"

As she rings up my order, swiping my credit card, she fills me in with more details. "I nearly fainted when he remembered me. God, he's swoon-worthy. But he only remembers me because you and I are tight."

She looks me right in the eye. "He asked how *you* were doing and wanted to know where *you* worked. Of course, I bragged you're *Southern Family Magazine's* top feature writer. He seemed impressed with that."

She takes a breath, "I asked if he was just visiting. He said he's settling down here for good. Isn't that great?"

She pushes my credit card to me. Numb, I pick it up and put it in my satchel.

"Oh, my god, I couldn't wait to tell you this morning. I wanted to text you right away, but this news needed to be told in person."

She fans herself. "I'm here to tell you, girlie. I nearly fainted! He is so," she mouths the word fucking, "fine!"

She's too distracted to notice Mario deliver my order to the counter, so he takes the opportunity to flirt, sliding it himself with a grin. "Good morning, Jorja."

She recovers, swatting his hand, then pushing him away. She slides my order to me. "Here you go, boo."

My hand shakes as I reach to scoop it up. Her hand grips my arm, stopping me. She leans in, determined, I know. "He has come back for you!"

I press my lips together, determined to deny it. "Don't be delusional, Macey."

"What?" Her mood dampens, and I sort of hate myself for it. She was so happy for me.

"You need to keep this real," I lecture her.

She crosses her arms and sets her jaw. "Are we going to have the kiss argument again?"

I cut my eyes to see if anyone is listening, then I lean forward and whisper through my clenched teeth. "That kiss was him satisfying his ego."

She shakes her head. "You were wrong then, and you are wrong now. That kiss was more than a kiss. It was..." She leans forward and whispers, "You know what that kiss was. It was everything a kiss is supposed to be, and he *has* come back for you. I saw it in his eyes when he asked about you."

God, I close my eyes in frustration, remembering that day. *Why does she make me relive it?*

"Macey, I was humiliated. He made sure everyone saw me melt, and then he left me standing there! It doesn't matter why he's back. I'm not HIS GIRL!"

She puts her hands on her hips. "I'm not wrong about this, Jorja."

I back away as I assure her. "Yes, you are."

She mouths, 'No, I'm not. He has come back for you!'

Jocko

When Lucifer and I walk into Dog Days, Demi Judson's dog grooming business, Demi pops off, "Well, look at you two studs!"

She walks around the counter, making a big deal about

sizing us up. Then she opens her arms. "Welcome home, Jocko. You look fantastic! SEAL service suits you."

Then she kneels and offers her hand for Lucifer to sniff. "Who's your beautiful boy?"

He offers his paw to shake, and she chuckles.

"Lucifer." I introduce him.

She cuts her eyes at me and laughs out loud. "Does Lucifer suit him?"

"Only in combat."

"He is beautiful!" She admires him as she shakes his paw. "Please tell me you're going to board him with me?"

"Maybe later. Right now, he's still adjusting to civilian life."

"Umm, I see." She nods as she scratches his chest. His lips curl, and his ears go limp in different directions as his eyes close in ecstasy. "Does that feel good, boy?"

"Apparently, it feels terrific." I laugh at him as a leg starts to quiver.

"I know how to please a man." She ruffles his fur, then stands up, puts her hands on her hips, and gives me a look that says that was an innuendo.

I smirk. Demi's easy on the eyes with legs that could wrap a man up in fantasies for a long, long time, and if it wasn't for Jorja, I would've tapped her way back when and be more than willing to take her up on that offer now, but....

"So, what brings you by if neither of those is your reason?" She smirks.

"I stopped by to ask if you had any dogs who could use some extra exercise. Lucifer and I run every morning, and he could use the socialization with other dogs."

"As a matter of fact, I do have a candidate. Ms. Jenkins has a high-strung Doberman, Tipper. How far do you run?"

"Five miles."

Her eyebrows raise. "That would bring Tipper's energy level down. What days and what time?"

"Every day at 5:00 a.m."

She looks me up and down again. "And that's why you look like you do."

"It's a contributing factor."

She walks around to the counter, takes a business card, flips it over, and writes on the back. "I'll speak to Ms. Jenkins. If she agrees, I'll work out the details for Tipper to join you. Maybe not every day, but three times a week. Give me a call in a couple of days."

"Excellent. Thanks, Demi."

"No problem." She hands the card to me. "I'm glad you're home in one magnificent piece."

"I have my boy to thank for that."

"You know, I'm a sucker for war stories." She tilts her head and raises her eyebrows.

"There are several to tell."

"How about knocking a few beers back with me Friday night at The Stallion? Say nine?"

I hesitate, and she laughs. "Bring Jorja. But if she turns you down? Well, I won't."

I snap my fingers and walk to the door, then pause and look back, grinning, "See you there."

At the truck, my phone rings. I load Lucifer as I answer, "Sup?"

"Jocko?"

"Yes, ma'am."

"This is Sandy Monroe, Greg's wife. Betty gave me your number. I hope you don't mind my calling."

"Hi, Sandy. Of course, not. I'm looking forward to meeting you."

"Likewise. Listen, I have an idea I would like to run by you."

"Sure. Shoot." I crank the truck and pull out of Dog Days, turning toward Dogwood Lane. When Sandy tells me what her idea is, I can't believe how perfect it is. "Oh, absolutely! I am all in," I inform her.

"Excellent! I'll set it up."

On the way, I get a group text from Aunt Betty. She's included all the brothers and their wives.

> Welcome Home Party for Jocko Tonight at 7.

I smile. *It is good to be home.*

When I pull into the vacant house next to Jorja's, Marianne is already there. She greets me at the door and walks me through the layout. It has three bedrooms and two baths. The kitchen is small, but the living room is large.

Lucifer wanders around, sniffing everything. But when we walk out onto the back porch, he bounds out into the big yard. I take his handball out of my pocket and throw it for him. He takes off after it at top speed.

Marianne stops chatting about all the benefits of this 'beauty' and asks, "Do you regret not following a career in baseball?"

I'm surprised by her question. It's so... unimportant. I look at her like she's crazy, and she laughs, uncomfortable and slightly embarrassed.

"No," I answer honestly. "Not a single second."

Lucifer returns with the ball, so I toss it up. He jumps,

snatching it out of the air, then hands it back to me to throw or toss again.

As I rear back to launch the ball long, she asks, "Do you know who your next-door neighbor is?"

I grin as I release it, then turn to look her dead in the eye. "Yes, I do."

She smiles as if I have given her a juicy tidbit of gossip, and I guess I have.

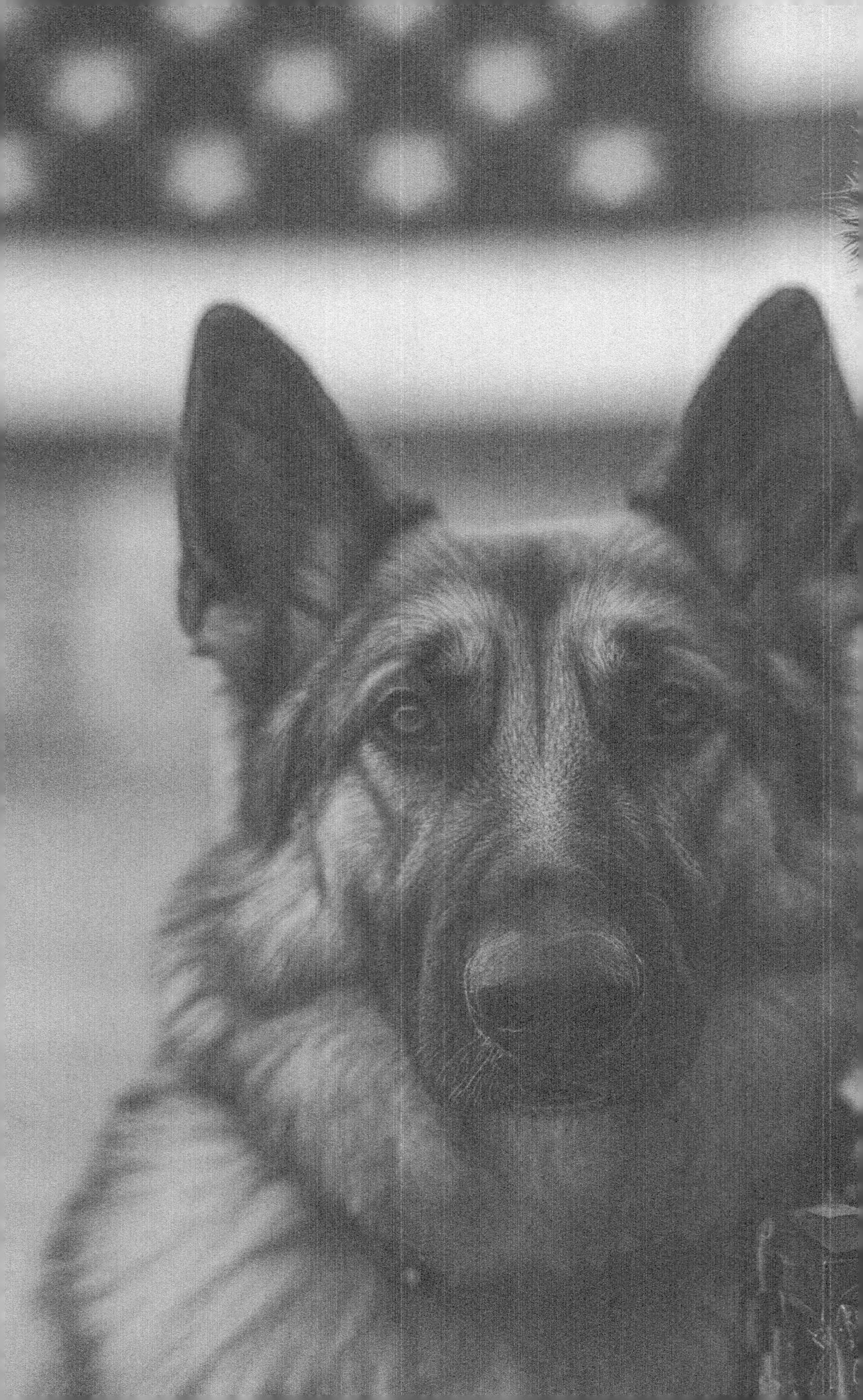

3

Jorja

Sitting at my desk at *Southern Family Magazine,* sipping my caffeine and fingering my cake, I remember the last moments of the last time I saw Jocko Monroe's cocky ass as if it were yesterday.

He was hovering possessively over me after planting a kiss on my lips that rocked my world, staring into my eyes, daring me to deny the desire coursing through my veins for him.

I couldn't. It was true. I wanted him to keep kissing me. To hold me. To cherish me. To claim me. But he didn't. He didn't say a word. He simply walked away. And left me standing there. With everyone gawking at me.

I was humiliated!

Afterward, I learned he had volunteered for the Navy. I was as surprised as everyone else. No one could believe he would give up a shot at playing professional baseball to serve in the military. But it was true. He had.

A couple of years later, I learned he had become a Navy SEAL, and I wondered if that was his reason.

I rub my lips, remembering the kiss.

Back then, everyone called it his goodbye kiss and gossiped about how we were passionately making out in the lockers. Even Joseph Pruitt got on board and told everyone that Jocko had threatened to beat his ass if he so much as looked at 'his girl' again.

After that, I couldn't even buy a date for the prom. No one would dare stand up to Jocko. No one wanted their ass beat over a girl like me. It didn't matter that he was off in the Navy. He would come home one day, and they feared that there would be hell to pay on that day.

Joseph put it in perspective for me. "Jorja, you're pretty and all, but you aren't worth the risk that I'll get my ass handed to me by Jocko."

No matter how hard I tried to tell everyone that he and I weren't involved, that he was just bullying me one last time before he left, no one believed me. Not even Macey, my best friend.

"Girl, don't pretend your toes weren't curling with that kiss! And don't pretend you weren't kissing him back! I saw you!"

What could I say? I was. But he wasn't. She didn't seem to see that. She only saw me melting for him.

The only person I ever convinced was my reflection in the mirror. She understood the depth of the humiliation he intentionally inflicted on me and the subsequent chaos his kiss caused in my life.

And now, Jocko's back.

hands. *I should be stoked about this assignment! This is a massive vote of confidence from Sandy. She trusts me to write our entry. This is a very big deal! There are ten magazines under Thompson Publishing. The competition is going to be steep.*

I drag my hands down my face, pulling my bottom lip. *But it's on fucking JOCKO! I can't avoid him now.*

An office group email arrives with the announcement.

Subject: Congratulations to Jorja Jones.

Sandy Monroe <Sandy@southernfamilymagazine.com>
8:45 a.m. (0 minutes ago)

To: Jorja <jorja@southernfamilymagazine.com>, Desiree <desiree@southernfa....

Good morning, staff. Please stop by Jorja's desk and offer your congratulations and best wishes. Jorja will be writing our entry into the First Annual Thompson Publishing House Contest.

I have chosen Heroes Among Us as our theme, and our very own Jocko Monroe will be featured. He returned yesterday after serving in the Navy as a SEAL.

Heroes Among Us will also be our theme for the upcoming summer months. Please submit your hero among us for consideration to be featured. We have space to honor ten.

Sandy

As one by one, the staff stops by my desk to congratulate and encourage me, I realize this is bigger than myself. This is about my work family and doing them proud.

I must overcome my personal issues with Jocko. I'll write a winning article, then walk away with my head held high.

I open my laptop and spend the rest of the day putting the finishing touches on the last feature article for this month's Spring Edition. Sorting through photos and placing some nice ones strategically throughout the layout page. I'm pleased with how I took a simple story on the flower stand that takes up the whole corner of town and transformed a humdrum topic into an article worthy of running as this edition's feature story. Sharing its origin as a lemonade stand a couple of decades ago and highlighting a few of the personal stories from the generations of owners it has had.

I sit back and critique my work one last time before sending it to Sandy for final approval and, hopefully, publication. "I like it," I tell myself, crossing my arms. "It's good."

A little voice in the back of my head says, 'This is why she chose you.'

I hit send, and "swoosh," it's off to Sandy for review.

Leaning back in my chair, stretching my arms over my head, and relaxing my shoulders and neck, I glance up at the clock on the wall. The red neon face reads 4:08—less than an hour to go.

I stand to stretch my back, and Desiree's head lifts to look over her laptop. She jumps to her feet, and as she rounds her desk. Britney sees her on the move and leaps to her feet too. The look on their faces as they descend on me says I'm about to be grilled, and I know the topic is Jocko.

I sit back down, cross my arms, and prepare to hold my head high and not whine or complain that my subject matter is the bully who I have had to deny having a romantic relationship with in high school for the last six years.

When they arrive, Britney hikes her hip and sits down on the edge of my desk. The thought that she wasn't as graceful as Sandy flits across my mind, but Desiree plants both palms in the center and leans over it to stare into my eyes, shoving the thought out.

My defenses go up with her assault despite my desire to remain open-minded.

"So?" Desiree asks.

"So ... what?" I ask, not sure if the grilling is about how I landed the contest assignment or Jocko's surprise return since we all went to school together, and they witnessed 'the goodbye kiss' firsthand.

Desiree cuts her eyes at Britney, then looks back down at me. "So ... *Jocko's* back in town."

I nod. *Of course, it would be about him.* "I heard."

They exchange a look, then she narrows her eyes and asks, "What do you mean, *you heard*? You haven't seen him yet?"

I shake my head. "No, I haven't."

They exchange another quick look, then race to the window. I stare after them, wondering what the heck they are looking for. Then they tell me, without telling me.

"I bet he's out there waiting for her!" Britney's voice is breathy and conspiratorial.

Desiree gushes emphatically. "Waiting to steal a Welcome Home kiss."

The blood drains from my face. *Oh, my god. He wouldn't dare!*

But then I take a breath ... *Calm down. Don't panic. We aren't in high school! He has no reason to be outside and no reason to bully me anymore. They still think he was kissing me goodbye, not that he was bullying me one last time before he left.*

The blood doesn't return to my face, though, and a sick feeling hits my stomach.

Britney fantasizes, "How romantic would that be?"

"I'll never forget watching him kiss her goodbye. I creamed my jeans." Desiree admits.

Britney adds, "And we wondered why he didn't hook up with any of us." She glances back at me and lowers her voice but intentionally doesn't whisper. "Jorja was fucking him the whole time."

I bite my lip, —*and just like that, the rumor returns.*

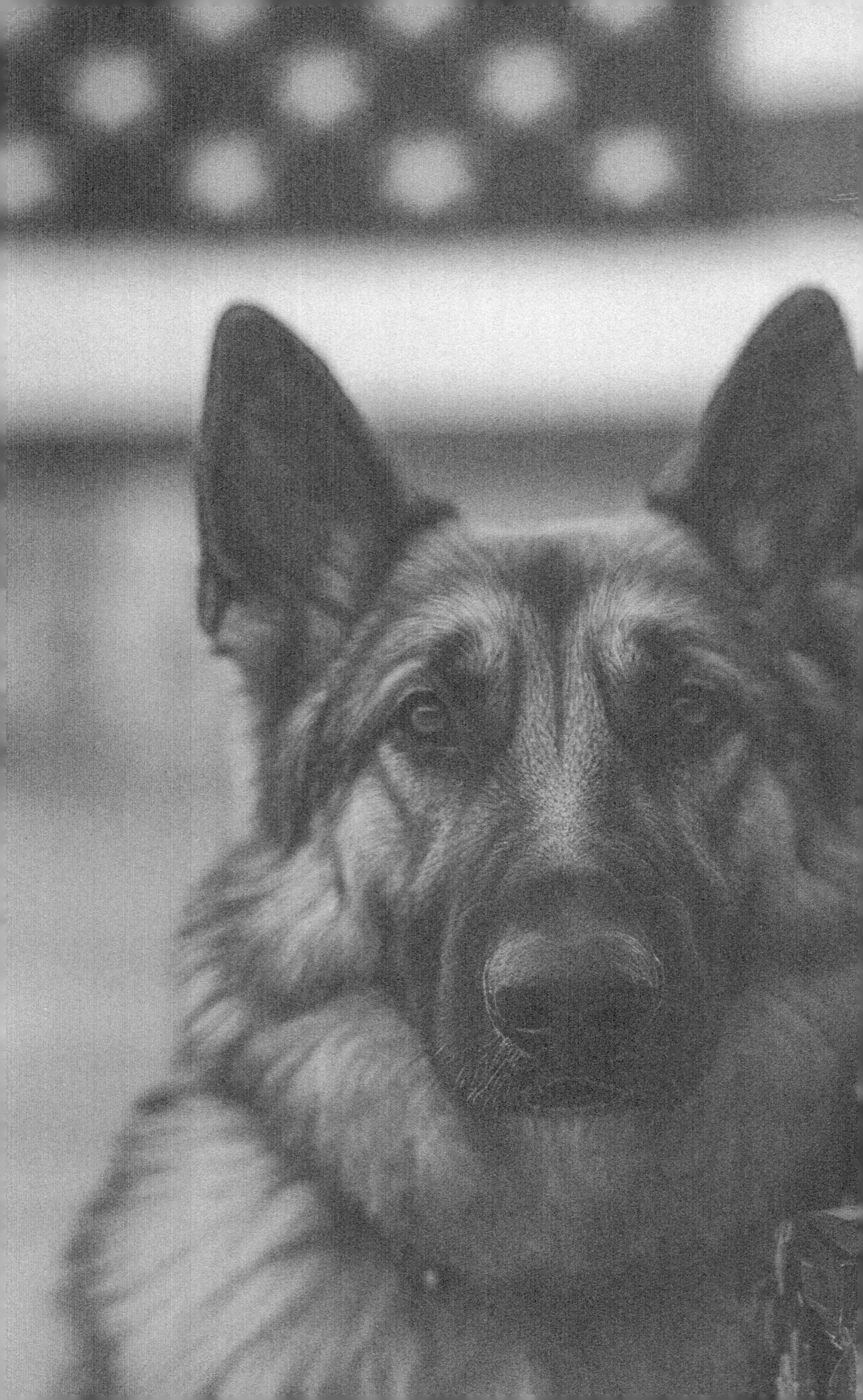

4

Jorja

Sandy snatches her office door open. She glances at Desiree and Britney at the window and notes that they aren't at their desks working. Then she points to me, "Grab your gear. We have to hurry."

Tossing my laptop in my satchel and then swinging it over my shoulder, I hurry around my desk to follow her.

"Has something happened?" I call after her.

She says as she slows down to push open the door, "I'll explain on the way." Then she sails right out the front entrance.

Hot on her heels, I glance up at the office window and see not only Desiree and Britney standing in it but a crowd of bodies. It looks like the entire staff is watching to see if Jocko is waiting to sabotage me.

The urge to stick my tongue out at them is replaced

with the thought of flipping them off. But I do neither. Sandy wouldn't understand, and I don't want her to.

I slide into the passenger seat and buckle my seatbelt. "What's up?"

She backs out of the parking spot. "Greg called to tell me to go ahead to his Mom's for dinner tonight. He was going to be late. Grace-Lifeline received a call that an Alzheimer's patient, a man in his seventies, is still missing in Jackson City. Apparently, he walked out of his home sometime during the night last night. They believe he's lost in the woods, and a hasty search today hasn't located him. They need to find him before the sun sets, so they're going to utilize a K9 to track him, and Greg's going to fly overhead in support of the search."

"Oh, wow! That's horrible. The poor man. The poor family. They must be worried sick."

"I told Greg the magazine is going to be featuring heroes among us this summer and asked if we can witness a rescue firsthand. He said yes, but we had to be there in 15 minutes."

My throat constricts, but I don't say a word. I'm afraid of flying.

We're almost to the airport when she asks, "Have you flown in a helicopter before?"

"No." I smile nervously at her.

"Don't worry. Greg's an excellent pilot."

I nod, knowing I can't wimp out, even if I want to.

"I know he is. I'll be fine." I try to sound convincing.

"If the helicopter's too much, you can join the ground search."

"That sounds like where the story will be. I'll do that." I change from my office attire to my workout clothes in the front seat as we fly down the road.

She laughs. "Your satchel's equipped for anything, I see."

I laugh as I remove my heels and put my Converse sneakers on. "I keep telling myself I'll go work out at the gym after work, but I never seem to make it over there."

When we arrive at Grace-Lifeline, the helicopter blades are already rotating at high speed. Ollie trots over as we open the car doors and step out.

"You made it just in time. Greg was about to lift off." He gives Sandy one of the headsets he has in his hand, and she takes off running to the helicopter. I admire how she manages to run in heels without turning an ankle.

"Here's your hearing protection," he states, but I don't take it. I look back at Sandy, she's putting hers on as she runs.

He closes the distance to me, pulls them open, and places them on my head. Then he's finding my ears and making sure they're covered. He pats my shoulder and mouths, "Go. Hurry. RUN!"

I take off running to the aircraft. As I close the distance, the helicopter grows. It's bigger than I thought it would be, and the noise is loud even with the headset on. Sandy's being lifted into it by a member of the crew. She disappears into the belly, and the crewman waits for me to arrive.

Ducking my head under the blades, I stop where she vanished and lift my arms. The crewman leans out, reaching for me, and I'm impressed with how massive he is. His big hands encircle my ribcage, and his strong arms lift my weight as if I weigh nothing.

Staring into his face shield, I see my wide-eyed, terrified expression. *Oh, Lord. I'm wearing my feelings on my face.*

He sets me down, and I focus on Sandy's calm demeanor, trying to draw courage from her. She pats the seat next to her as the crewman closes the door behind me. I sit, slamming my eyes shut tight.

As loud as the helicopter was, it gets even louder as the engine winds up, then it begins to vibrate, then shakes. The massive man sits next to me, and his body spills over into my space. He pulls my headset off one ear and shouts, "SEATBELT."

I nod but can't move.

He leans against me as he reaches over, carelessly bumping my boobs, then he begins playing with my ass, and I let him. Too scared to even try to help.

Now, he's fondling my lap! I peer through my squinted eyelids to see who's practically molesting me, but his visor's still down, shielding his face.

Concerned I'm being groped, but not so much that I stop him, I watch his long fingers secure my seatbelt. When it clicks, he gives me a thumbs-up as his torso retreats to lean back in his seat. I cut my eyes as I nod and catch a glimpse of his smirking profile.

I don't care that you find my fear funny. I am scared, shitless.

I stare down at the floor directly in front of me and pray I'll manage to fly with some semblance of dignity.

The helicopter lurches up to a hover.

My body seizes, and all hope of dignity vanishes. I'm terrified!

My hands shoot out to grab hold of the seat, thrusting themselves down and latching on. I hit my mark beside Sandy because she's small, but I miss on the other side. The huge dude's hard leg makes my hand skip off, and it shoots between his legs. Uncaring that I'm now the one molesting him, I grope his crotch, searching for the seat to anchor myself.

As the aircraft lurches forward, then lifts, airborne, I

squeeze what I hope is the seat edge. The pitch of the climb freezes my terrified position. But moments turn to seconds, and I realize that my hand's not gripping the seat edge. I've grabbed his dick, and I'm helpless to let go.

The helicopter banks hard to the left, and I scream as my body slams against Mr. Big Dick. He lifts his arm and pulls me in tight to cuddle, and I hide my face against him.

His scent is woodsy, musky, clean, and even though I'm scared to death —*My god, the man smells good! Very masculine. Very manly.*

He holds me tight, offering comfort. I take a deep breath and try to relax, but —*his cock is growing bigger, longer, harder!*

Oh. My. God! How embarrassing for him and for me! Geez, Jorja! Let go! You're choking it!

I try, but I can't! I am too terrified!

Fuuuuuck! I want to die!

He squeezes my shoulder, offering comfort, and I resign myself to the fact that I'll apologize later for being such a big 'fraidy cat, but I'm owning it right now.

At altitude, we level off, and the flight becomes relatively smooth. Sandy taps me on the shoulder, but I don't let go of my security blanket. I turn my face to look at her.

She leans forward so I can read her lips. "Are you okay?"

I nod, confirming I am. *But I am not. I am so not!*

She glances at the man holding me and gives him a knowing smile, then pulls her phone out of her pocket and begins taking pictures. I know I should be doing that, but I'll just have to beg her forgiveness for being a big baby later.

Then the helicopter descends, dropping fast. My stomach tries to roll over, and I ball up, trying desperately not to puke.

The poor dude pulls me so tight against him that my tits feel like they are about to pop out of my bra. I lay my head on his muscular chest and let him hold me. Again, his manly scent overwhelms my thoughts, and as his hand softly strokes my arm, I realize he's making me wet!

Geez-us! Jorja! Now? Christ! I close my eyes, mortified at my body's reaction, only to visualize the ginormous cock I'm clutching.

Then the helicopter slows as quickly as it dropped from the sky, bounces slightly, and we've landed.

He continues to hold me close, shielding my hand's position, and I slowly release my fingers, freeing his cock.

Not wanting to know who the man with the big dick is but needing to apologize and thank him, I lift my face off his chest and look at him, saying, "Thank you, and I'm so sorry about that."

But my breath vanishes as the truth I've tried so hard to deny for six years, seventeen days, and approximately two hours lays bare my broken heart. Then it pounds to life inside my chest, rejoicing at the sight as an all too familiar, devilishly wicked grin spreads across perfectly sculpted lips.

I stare, frozen again in fear, as that mouth with those delicious lips forms the words, "Sup, Juicy?"

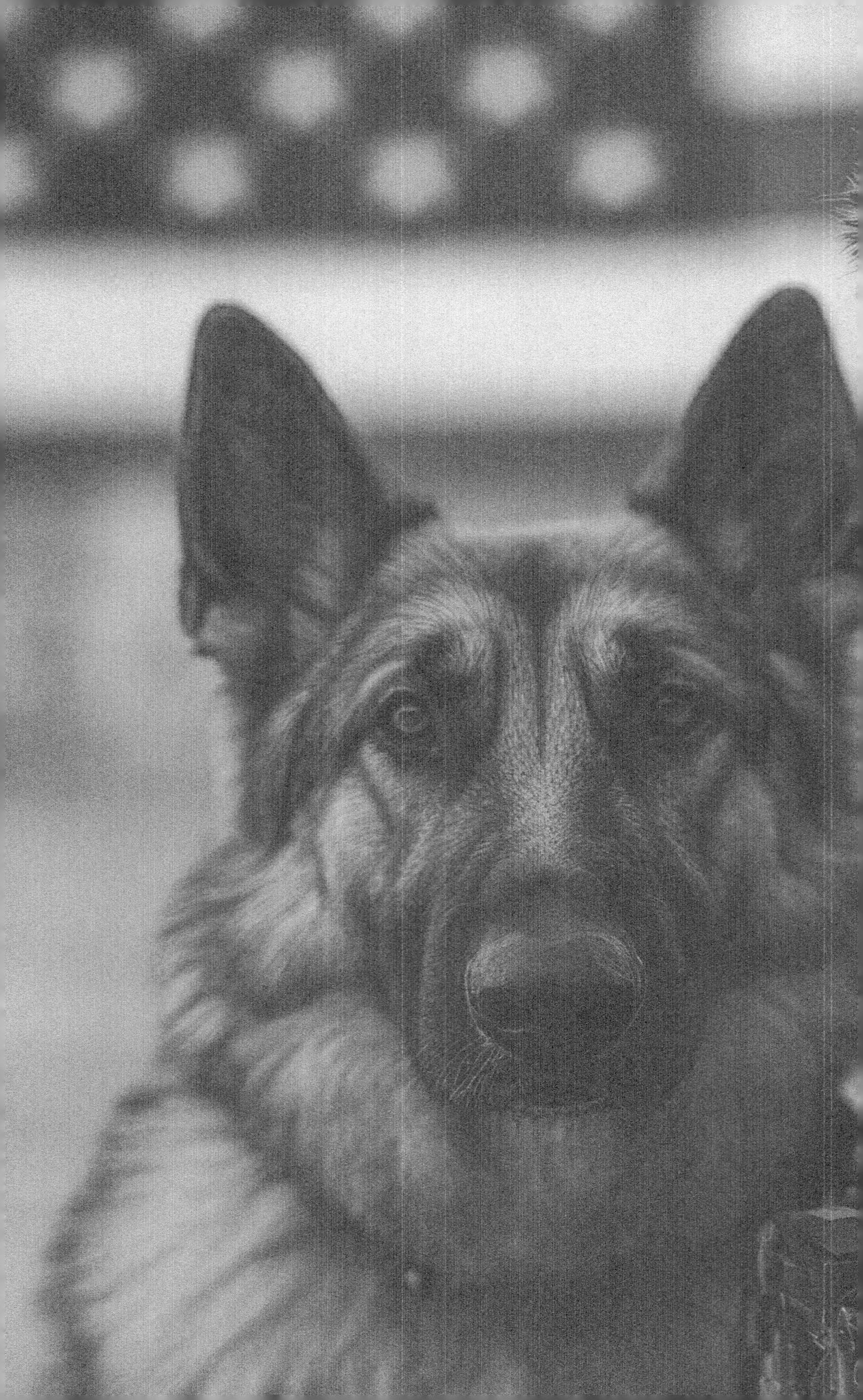

5

Jorja

My mouth waters as his mesmerizing tongue licks those perfect lips and turn my insides to mush.

Jocko's arm gently releases his hold on me as he smiles at my stunned face.

Oh. My. God. I can't believe it.

Unbuckling his belt, he slides out of the seat to a crouch. Unable to take my eyes off him, staring completely gobsmacked, knowing he's loving that but unable to control it, I absorb every detail.

Macey was right. He is huge! A fucking stud! All filled out, and ALL MAN! Oh, dear lord! I am doomed!

Another crew member moves to the door, and Jocko, hunched over because he's way too tall to stand, walks over to wait for it to open.

I'm shocked to see a dog was sitting next to him. He's wearing a blue visor, ear protection, and a military vest with a harness holding some high-tech equipment. Sitting calmly, focused solely on Jocko. He's solid black, beautiful, and totally badass in his gear!

The reason I'm here is because Jocko and his dog are the ones tracking the missing man. Sandy touches my arm, smiles, and starts helping me unbuckle my seatbelt. I glance back at him, but I can't tell if he's looking at his dog or me until he gives a very masculine head nod.

My tummy flip-flops as an embarrassed grin slides across my face while a sexy as fuck grin spreads across his.

It was his cock I was holding, and holy shit, what a dick!

He slides the helicopter door open as the engine winds down and jumps out.

Doing my job, I note that his whole demeanor has changed. He's no longer an arrogant baseball player. The man jogging toward a group approaching the helicopter moves fluidly with grace and power, oozing competence and confidence.

Geez-ma-neez! He is fine! Straight legs, thick thighs, nice tight ass, culminating with thick broad shoulders.

Sandy taps my arm, and I pull my eyes off Jocko's magnificence to look at her. Her eyes are twinkling, and I know she set me up. I smirk as she shouts, "GO. You're on the ground with Jocko."

I nod, then crawl to the edge of the aircraft. As I swing my legs over and prepare to jump down, I scan the area. We've landed in a field behind a house. There are cop cars in the drive. As well as an ambulance, plus a score of other vehicles. A relatively large group of people are watching as a small group walks out to meet Jocko.

When he arrives, he takes his helmet off and runs his hand through his hair. The familiarity of that old habit sends a little jolt through me, and the past six years fade away.

Shaking hands, the men speak to each other, and several of them point toward the woods. Jocko raises his arm, then drops it. The K9 bolts, leaping out of the helicopter and runs full speed to him as the small group of men return to the larger group.

The blades start to rotate faster as the engine begins to wind back up.

Oh, crap! I jump down and run across the field.

When the dog reaches Jocko, he sits, focused on every move his handler makes. The degree of trust and devotion is evident and impressive. I've never been around a working dog before.

Jocko kneels next to him to remove his flight gear. He stores the items in his backpack and glances back. A flash of pearl-white teeth shines against his tanned skin when he sees me running to him.

Jocko

Jorja's mop of dirty blonde hair blows around her face as the wind from the helicopter lifting off swirls around us. She's wearing straight-leg, tie-dyed yoga shorts and a matching U-shape sports top with her toned mid-drift exposed. As her shapely legs carry her to me, her tits bounce playfully from side to side. The hard-on from holding her in the helicopter isn't given a reason to ease off. Her body's better than I remember. She's all woman. All grownup. Curvy, full figure. On a scale of one to ten, she's a ten times ten.

I stand as she arrives, towering over her, and enjoy the view of her beautiful ample breasts from this vantage point. She's out of breath, so they're surging up and down.

Ummm, I've literally whacked off to that vision hundreds of times.

A grin plasters itself on my face, and she tries not to smile, but it flirts with her features as her big amber eyes, framed by perfectly arched brows, roll around looking for somewhere to land other than my grinning face, embarrassed she was clutching my cock.

I reach for her head, and she stiffens, then her eyes lock onto mine. The memory of the last time I held her sparks between us, and the urge to kiss her is overwhelming. I let my eyes tell her how much I want to, but this isn't the time nor the place.

"You aren't going to need these now." I gently ply her headset off, trying not to pull her hair. Her face softens as she submits, and I promise myself that I'll see that look again as she moans with pleasure. I have six years of fantasies to fulfill with her, and I intend to complete every last one.

"We need to get going. The sun's setting and daylight is fading." I tell her as I kneel next to my backpack and stuff her headset inside. "I recommend you ride the mule with the sheriff."

Her eyes widen. "Mule?"

"It's an ATV, all-terrain vehicle, a jazzed-up golf cart if you will." I stand and hoist the bag on my back with a bounce.

"Oh ... but I ...."

Hooking Lucifer's twenty-foot lead onto his collar, I

smirk. "Don't worry, City Mouse. You won't miss a thing. You'll be right behind me."

"Okay." She nods, and Lucifer leads the way to the search party.

Jorja

DING! A text hits my phone. It's from Sandy.

> Don't forget to take pictures.

> DON'T WORRY. I'M ON THE GROUND NOW. LOL.

Jocko dips his broad shoulders, letting the backpack swing to the ground as the sheriff holds out a plaid shirt. "Mr. Romano wore this yesterday."

He takes it as he nods at me. "Jorja's with you."

"Sure." The sheriff reaches down to grab the backpack. "I can take this too." He gives it a tug, but it barely budges. "What do you have in here? Bricks?"

Jocko laughs as he scoops it up, carries it to the mule, and sets in down in the back. "Gear."

He looks at me. "You all set?"

I nod. "Good luck."

"We don't need luck. We need a good scent."

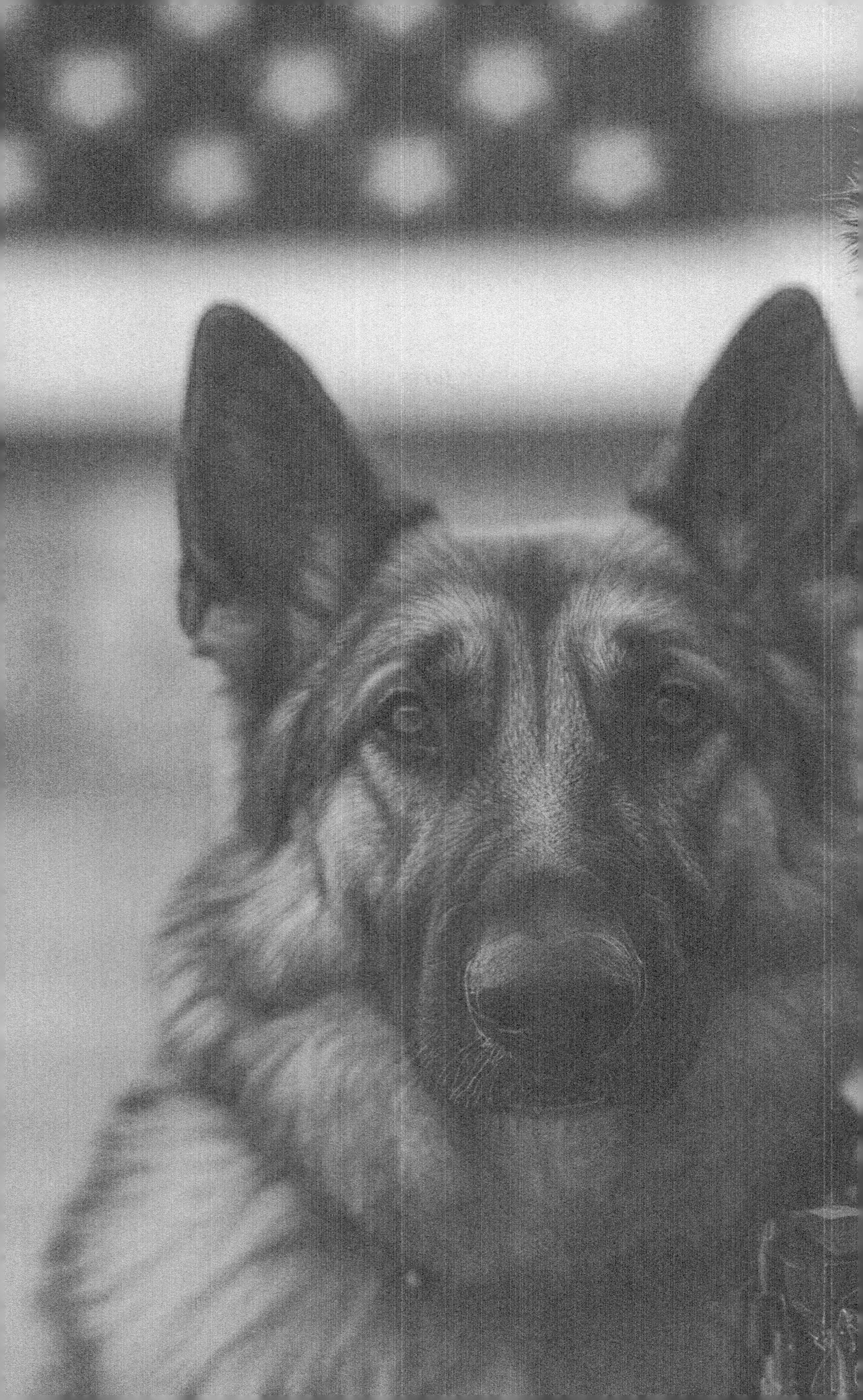

6

Jorja

Seated in the mule, phone camera at the ready with the search team gathered around, I watch Jocko take charge. He gives them a quick overview of what the dog will do and instructs them to stay behind, out of the way. It's important to preserve the scent. Then he says, "No man left behind. Let's go bring Mr. Romano home."

A couple of "oorahs" follow as he leans down, holds the shirt with the man's scent for the dog to sniff, then gives him the command to "track."

The K9's nose goes straight to the ground. He takes off across the field we landed in.

The sheriff gives the mule gas, and we follow behind. "I sure hope that dog isn't taking us on a wild goose chase and he can find the old man. We combed these woods this morning."

We follow along silently for a few minutes. "Jocko's a

Navy SEAL," I state, hoping to instill confidence. The Sheriff seems genuinely concerned for the well-being of the lost man.

His mouth turns down at the corners with an 'is that so' expression and the worry in his eyes clears somewhat. "That explains a lot."

"I thought it might."

"I got a call around 3:30 from Chief Kent in Live Oak, and he offered Jocko and his K9 to help us out. It'll be a miracle if they can find him, though."

Watching Jocko and his K9 work impresses the hell out of me. Jocko gives him the full rein, running beside and behind him but letting the dog work independently of commands. The dog stays focused, and its pace is brutal. The rest of the search team spans out on their ATV four-wheelers, keeping a safe distance behind.

As we ride, the sheriff asks why I'm here. "How come you're tagging along?"

"I'm a journalist, and I'm doing an article on Heroes Among Us. Jocko is my subject."

"Ah! That makes sense, then."

After about twenty minutes, Jocko stops and waves us over. The sheriff pulls alongside him. "Did you lose the scent?"

Jocko is breathing hard and sweating, but he answers as he walks to the back. "No. We need to hydrate. The pace is fast."

"Yes, it is. Impressive." The sheriff acknowledges.

I spin around to watch Jocko as he unzips his backpack, takes out a couple of bottles of water, a bowl, and serves his dog first. As the K9 laps up the liquid, Jocko smiles at me and winks.

My heart does a flip-flop, and my tummy bottoms out. *Man, alive, that wink!*

I quickly raise the camera to hide the expression that spread involuntarily across my face. Nothing good will come of letting him see my reflexive reaction! I don't need to encourage him!

He lifts a bottle to those perfectly sculpted lips and watching them pucker in the zoomed screen makes my clit feel like butterflies are fluttering around it. I sigh as I try to ignore my reaction. *I'm just like every other girl.*

Mesmerized by his Adam's apple working the liquid down his throat as he swallows, I snap pictures, covering my clit chaos. When it's drained, he lowers it, and I pinch the screen to zoom out.

His body fills the screen, so I snap more pictures to capture his posture. The way he stands is impressive. Majestic even. His posture is proud but also unassuming. Everyone here knows he's in command without him saying a word.

My emotions fight as I admire him and at the same time, resent him.

His pumped chest challenges the stretch of his shirt. His bulked shoulders taper sharply to his trim waist. His straight legs are big as tree trunks and belie his agility. His gracefulness as he sprinted through the woods, dodging bushes, jumping fallen trees, and ducking under low-hanging branches, was like a dance with nature. The terrain, though, was a true obstacle course, and he maneuvered it effortlessly. Well, not effortlessly. He was out of breath and had broke a sweat, but it was poetry in motion —harmony.

He stuffs the empty bottles they drained into his backpack, and the attention to such a small detail impresses me.

He's conscientious about the environment. I snap more pictures as he stuffs them in his backpack. Then he bends over and retrieves his K9's bowl.

The thickness of his broad back curves sharply downward to his trim waist and then flares dramatically with his full, round ass.

I snap more pictures. Documenting his every move.

It strikes me that the genetically gifted boy in high school has grown up to be a beautiful beast of a man. Then and now, the "it" factor oozes from every fiber of his masculine presence.

And that's why women fawn over him. Including me.

Ready to return to the search, he offers the old man's shirt for the dog to sniff and changes his command to "Find."

The K9 takes off, and Jocko matches his pace, stride for stride.

As we follow a safe distance behind, I ask the sheriff, "How far do you think we've come?"

"Well," he ponders a moment, "they've been running for over twenty minutes, so ... two miles, I'd reckon." He glances at me.

"Did your search extend this far out?" I ask as he slows to avoid a fallen tree.

"No, we didn't think the old man could make it this far. He's feeble."

Suddenly, Jocko's dog changes direction and pulls hard against the lease, lunging for more slack, wanting to run faster. Jocko adjusts and kicks his speed into another gear, letting him sprint.

The sheriff excitedly offers hope. "Maybe they found him." He pushes harder on the gas pedal for more speed, and I'm forced to grip the overhead handhold to stay seated as the ATV bounces and lunges through the woods.

Jocko vanishes from sight. The terrain thickens, and we slow down.

Then we hear Jocko yell, "STAY!"

I spot him through the trees just as his arms come together over his head, and he dives headfirst out of sight. His body stretched in flight, every muscle tense but lengthened. Again, I'm caught off guard by how beautifully masculine he is and —how different now.

The sheriff corrects his distance as we slow and break out of the tree line. "Make that two and a half miles. We're at the riverbank."

Before the mule comes to a complete stop, I jump out and run to the edge of the embankment to stand next to his dog. He had instantly obeyed. Stopping and sitting, but he shakes with every fiber of his being, yearning to be by Jocko's side.

Looking across the water, I spot Jocko power swimming across the river's current with a smooth, steady, strong free stroke. The sight is impressive.

I snap some pictures.

The man they have been searching for is clinging onto a tree branch stuck in an eddy in the middle of the river.

I hold my breath. Fearful for what happened to him and fearful for what's about to happen. The danger is obvious! For everyone involved!

The sheriff comes alongside me and cusses, "Damn!" Then he keys the radio. "We've found Mr. Romano. He's in the river. We're just below the bridge at Horseshoe Bend."

"Roger that." Greg's voice answers. "En route."

The ATVs begin arriving, and the other searchers line up with us on the riverbank to watch.

Jocko stops just short of the old man in a calm area below the eddy and treads water, assessing the situation. Then he dives under, and my heart pauses its beating. He surfaces on the other side of the fallen tree, and the old man turns his head to look at him.

Then Mr. Romano throws his head back *and laughs.*

I make a mental note to ask Jocko what he said to him to ease the tension.

Jocko waves to us, then gives a thumbs up, signaling that Mr. Romano is alright. My breath returns, but my heart is still tight with the tension.

The chopping noise from the rotary blades arrives before we see the helicopter break the tree line.

"I see him." Greg's voice squawks over the radio.

He pilots the Grace-Lifeline aircraft a short distance down the river where the bank meets the shallow water and hovers, staying high enough that the downwash from the rotor blades doesn't create more water issues for Jocko and Mr. Romano. Several rescuers start working their way down there to the shoreline.

Jocko watches everything unfolding. They must be talking because I can see his beautiful smile even from this distance, and my heart flip-flops again.

Then he dives under the surface, comes up next to Mr. Romano, hooks an arm over the man's chest, rolls him over onto his back, and swims with the current across the river with Mr. Romano in tow to the shallow water, where the helicopter hovers.

The down draft of the blades stirs the trees' tops and creates a rippling effect across the water. I can clearly see Greg and Charles in the cockpit, and a crew member sits on the deck with his legs hanging out. I know Sandy's inside, but she isn't visible.

As Jocko approaches, two rescuers wade out and wait in position as the Grace-Lifeline rescue basket begins to descend to them.

When Jocko reaches the shallow water, I gasp in appreciation for a body built like that and his willingness to risk it all for a total stranger in need. His wet clothes are plastered to his perfect physique as he emerges with all the glory of Aquaman.

Waist deep in the water, he squats and picks the man up into his arms, cradling him as he sloshes up the river to where the men are holding the rescue basket steady.

When he arrives, he gently places the old man inside, shakes his hand, and pats him on the back. Then he laughs out loud with the other guys at something the old man's said. He takes a couple of steps back, looks up at the helicopter, and gives Grace-Lifeline the thumbs-up signal.

Immediately, they begin hoisting the old man up, and he starts waving to us. Of course, we all wave back.

Watching Mr. Romano being safely loaded into the helicopter, I look around and realize who the heroes among us are. They're the men and women who unselfishly give to others, and I've never been more proud of anything in my entire life!

A couple of seconds after, the old man disappears into the helicopter, the door shuts, and Grace-Lifeline flies away. Then, Jocko and the rescuers head to the bank to return to us.

I'm overwhelmed with a mix of emotions. Seeing Jocko in this environment, has me totally confused as to who he is and how I should respond to him. Obviously, he isn't the cruel bully anymore, but.... I don't know.

As Jocko gets closer, his dog's tail wags so hard it sweeps the ground, clearing off the leaves. But he doesn't break his position. He's in the exact spot where he was when he was given the command to stay. The discipline applied to continue to obey is as impressive as the obedience to the initial command. His front paws begin dancing with excitement, and I capture his happy paw dance on video.

Everyone watching claps as Jocko arrives, and he casually glances around at them. I get the impression he's a bit embarrassed by their applause. He gestures acknowledgment with his hand, 'I hear ya, but it isn't necessary,' and then sucks his lips and calls his K9. "Come 'ere, boy!"

In three lunges, the dog is there, encircling his legs, with all four paws prancing with excitement, rubbing Jocko's legs affectionately like a cat. Jocko drops to one knee, heaps praise on him and gives the dog's body a roughhouse petting. "That's my boy! What a good man! Good job, Lucifer. You are the man! Love you, buddy."

I start to laugh. His name is Lucifer. Why am I not surprised?

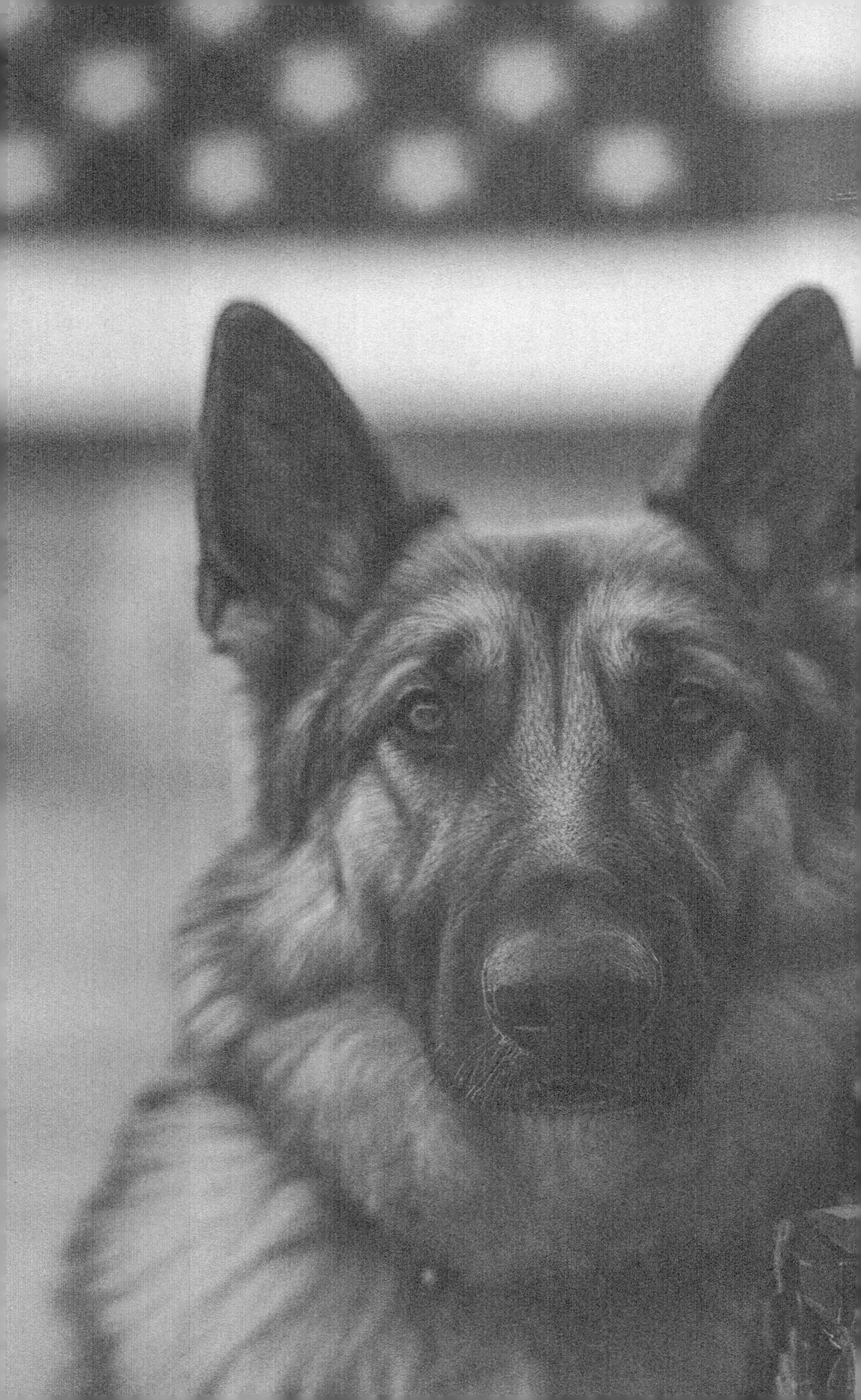

7

Jocko

___

The sheriff and the rescue team walk up with their hands outstretched and big grateful grins on their faces. "Congratulations, man. We appreciate you helping out."

I shake their hands. "No problem. Glad to be of service."

As the men take turns giving Lucifer the attention and praise he deserves, I take my shoes off and pour water out of them. Then remove my shirt and wring it out. I walk over to the mule where Jorja's retreated to wait. Her eyes are glued on me, and that's precisely where I want them to be.

Opening my backpack, I remove a towel and a change of clothes. Modesty isn't a quality I've ever possessed. I'm soaked and cold, and since Jorja's the only female here, I begin peeling my pants off.

"God!" She lunges for the towel to hide her face, and her panic makes me laugh.

"What's the matter, Juicy? Afraid of seeing my boner?"

"OOOooo, you're so infuriating! Why do you torture me?"

"I thought we settled that years ago. Because I can ... and because you're so damn delicious when you get all pissed off."

Stepping out of my wet pants, I wring the water out of them. The sound from the splash draws a peek-a-boo out from behind the towel, and she moans as she hides her face again. Her words are muffled when she says, "Dear LORD! Are you always so insolent?"

"Insolent? Because I'm not embarrassed?" I gently pull on the towel, and her grip tightens. But I drag it down until her eyes lock on mine. "I'm supposed to dry off with this." I grin at her, and her eyes flare, afraid of seeing what she tried to squeeze the life out of earlier.

I snatch it away like ripping a bandaid off, and she gets an eyeful of my giant cock.

Laughing, I tease her as I wrap it around my waist. "Or because I'm brazen."

She scrunches her eyes so hard that her nose crinkles. "God, Jocko! Why do you harass me?"

"Harass you? That's harsh, Juicy, I'm hurt. What have I ever done to harass you?"

"Really? That nickname alone is harassment."

"Juicy isn't a derogatory word. We both know it's true and if it's true, you can say it. Therefore, it's not harassment." I smirk at her, and her eyes narrow. "Have you missed me?" I lean down and whisper, "I've missed you."

Her hand shoots out and plants itself firmly on my chest. "No. I haven't missed you!"

"Ah, I'm hurt." I chuckle as I position myself to kiss her.

"What do you think you are doing?"

"I'm going to kiss you."

"No, you're not! You aren't going to bully me anymore!"

I'm taken aback by her tone, and stand up, forgetting about the kiss. The word 'bully' stings. I frown at her, confused she's thought so. "Bully you? I've never bullied you."

"What exactly do you call the way you treated me then?"

My mouth goes slack, and words evaporate.

"You're 'kiss'," she spits, "humiliated me in front of the whole school!" She announces, crossing her arms. Then her lips press into a hard straight line.

My head tilts, and my brows furrow as I study her posture and expression. *She's dead serious.*

Taking a step back, I ask. "What are you talking about? I haven't harassed you. Nor have I bullied you. And I, sure as hell, never humiliated you."

Her jaw sets in anger. "You are infuriating!"

I drop all pretense of play now. We aren't children. We're adults.

"Clear the air, Jones. Explain. I'm fucking clueless about what you're talking about." I command her, not harshly, but firmly.

"Your goodbye!" She shakes her head and looks away.

"What about it?" I cross my arms, matching her posture.

She grits her teeth. "You *forced* your kiss on me."

I clear my throat, offended she used the word forced in the first place but also emphasized it.

I respond indignantly, correcting her recollection. "We *shared* a passionate kiss. Don't try to deny it. You enjoyed the hell out of it."

She bites her bottom lip, confirming she did, but she doesn't relinquish her perception. Not wanting to push her further away, I soften my tone and decide to concede the point to her. I did catch her off guard, and I was angry that Joseph Pruitt was moving in on her when I was leaving. I unfold my arms and say, "Okay, I'll admit it. Maybe I did."

She looks over at the men playing with Lucifer, but she isn't seeing them. She's processing. "Fine. I'll admit it too. I enjoyed it. There. Happy?" She cuts her eyes, shooting daggers at me. And dammit, my cock hardens, and I'm thankful the towel is hiding it. Her feisty sparring has always turned me on. She looks away again, hurt. "But it was humiliating!"

Truly flabbergasted, I put my hands on my hips. "I'm confused, Babe." She glances at me with the endearment, and I ask, "Explain how a kiss that is earth-shattering can be humiliating?"

She bites her bottom lip again. Then she takes a deep breath, and the look she gives me pins me to the ground. I couldn't move even if I wanted to.

"You're right. The kiss was earth-shattering. It rocked my world. But I didn't want it rocked! Especially by you! You were arrogant, and you were an asshole." She shakes her head, and her layered hair sways around her beautiful face. "And what I feared happened. Just like all the other girls in school, I couldn't resist you either. I melted in your arms in front of everyone! Then ..." She looks away, not allowing me to look into her eyes. "You left me standing there without saying a word. How was I supposed to feel?"

I lean back on my heels. *Fuck! I fucked that up!* Stunned speechless, I rub my scruff, absorbing her unbelievable reaction.

She spews her truth. "It was humiliating! *I* was humiliated. *You* humiliated *me*." Her face glares at me. "Now, after six years, seventeen days, and two hours, plus or minus a few minutes," she sasses. "Since that kiss with ZERO communication." She holds up her hand, forming a '0' for emphasis. "You expect me to fall at your fucking feet? I don't think so!"

Two things happen to me the moment I hear her confession that she's counted the days. One, I'm confident she's mine. No one holds a grudge that long without love being involved, and no one counts the days unless they are devastated by the loss of it. It's been ten years and two months since my parents passed. And two, her tone and her posture piss me off. I would never expect her to 'fall at my fucking feet!'

I grab a handful of her hair to hold her face still so I can look her in the eye, and she will hear every word of truth I say to her. I don't do drama. I never have. Life is too fucking short.

Her eyes spit daggers at me, and she tries to pull away. But I'm claiming her. Right here. Right now!

"Jorja, I fucked up. I'll own that. I'll even apologize for humiliating you. That was never my intention. The truth is ... I went back to school that day just to say goodbye to you."

Her eyes stay steady on my face. Her expression unchanged.

"I didn't go that day to kiss you. I really didn't know the depth of my own feelings until I saw Joseph Pruitt make a move on you. That's when I knew I was fucked, and I wasn't prepared for it. I realized that if I didn't kiss you right then, I might not have the opportunity *ever* again, and I would regret it for the rest of my life."

Her eyes soften slightly, and I reduce the tension of my grip on her hair. "That if I didn't kiss you right then, you would never know how I felt about you, and you, sure as hell, wouldn't wait for me to come home. You would go on with your life, and I would've missed my opportunity to be a part of it. So, I seized the opportunity before I thought it through. That's why I forced a kiss on you."

Her eyes soften more.

"Then, fuck. As soon as my lips touched yours, all the feelings for you I had been stifling burst forth like a dam breaking. It was overwhelming. I had found you and would lose you within minutes, and I was too choked up to physically speak."

She blinks back tears.

"I should've contacted you, but I didn't know what to say, and once I walked onto the base, my life belonged to the Navy. I haven't spoken to a single person outside of my family from Live Oak. But I kept tabs on you."

I release her hair and cup her face. "I apologize for not communicating with you directly. I should have. All I can do now is ask for your forgiveness for not getting in touch with you. If I had known you were suffering, I would've come home and told you face to face."

I stroke her cheek with my thumb. "I apologize that you've spent the last six years confused. I've spent the last six years cherishing that kiss. It shook my foundation. I never stopped thinking of you. Never stopped hoping you would be waiting for me to return. And the memory of that earth-shattering kiss is the only thing that got me through the darkest, hardest times."

I pinch her chin and hold her face steady as I lean in. "Jorja, I'm not an immature boy now."

She smirks, and my heart has hope.

"I'm a man who's come home, hoping to pick up where I thought we left off."

"Which is?" She whispers.

"Which is to my girl who's ready to explore the spark that kiss ignited and see if we can build a solid relationship."

Her eyes close, and her brows furrow.

"Don't shut me out. Look at me."

She opens them and stares with wonder at my face.

"That being said, the first thing you need to understand about who the man Jocko Monroe is ... is that I would never expect you to fall at my fucking feet. I don't want a doormat. I want a woman who stands beside me. Who walks with me. I want a mate to share my life with."

The fight in her amber eyes vanishes. All I see there now is a willingness to try.

I run my thumb over her lips and smile. "Do you know what's about to happen?" I nod for her. "That's right. I'm going to kiss you again. Do you know why?"

I rake my eyes over her voluptuous body as my cock pushes against the towel. "Because I really want to taste your sweetness. And we both know what's going to happen when I kiss the fuck out of your mouth. You're going to kiss the fuck out of mine. Because deep down inside," I trace a finger down her neck to the fabric that covers her breast, and little goosebumps rise to the surface, "you've been waiting for me to come home, wanting another earth-shattering kiss to rock your fucking world."

I slide my hand back into her hair and pull her head back by it as I close the gap between us. Towering over her, dominating her, I whisper, "So, Juicy, get ready. This is me kissing you because I want you, and I promise I'm never leaving you again."

Submission stares up at me, and that is an addictive drug.

I press my lips lightly on hers, nibbling little caressing

butterfly kisses until she arches her back, slides her arms up my chest, around my neck, and kisses the fuck out of my mouth.

The taste of her is sweeter than I remember. Her essence fills all the hollow parts of my soul, and I know I've made it home.

When I let her go, we are both breathless, and we are bonded. The past is forgiven, and the future is what we make it.

I stare down into her eyes and tease her. "As much as I would much rather continue kissing you." I back up. "Moving my lips from one delicious part of your body to another." I drop the towel and launch it at her. "The next time I kiss you, I'll show you just how brazen I am."

The towel hits her squarely in the face.

Jorja

I hold the towel over my face as Jocko changes clothes. My mind races with everything he said. My heart believes him. My body wants him. But my mind is confused.

Trust is an issue for me. As much as I don't want to admit it, it is.

When I was seven years old, my father left my mother. Like every little girl, I loved my daddy. But not because he was involved in my life, only because he was my daddy.

I never asked my mom why he left. In the beginning, I assumed it was all her fault. She drove him away. A normal reaction when she was always the one yelling and accusing him of not loving her and loving someone named Dolores.

The night he left, he came into my bedroom and kissed me, not goodnight, but goodbye. I cried and begged him to take me with him, but he said he couldn't. Dolores didn't want children. I had to stay with Mommy. And although he promised to come back to visit, he never did.

My mom was always honest with me about what happened. She didn't want me to distrust men. She wanted me to marry and have babies. But she didn't want me to have my heart broken either.

She decided the best way to teach me about love was to watch "Meeting Joe Black" over and over again.

I think that's why I didn't want to fall for Jocko in the first place. Because every girl wanted him, and I was afraid one of them would be a Dolores.

"I'm dressed, Jorja. You can stop hiding behind the towel."

I lower it and smirk at him. He holds his hand out, and I toss it to him. He stuffs it in the backpack and says, "I need to schmooze with the guys."

I take a seat in the mule to wait. Watching him interact with them makes me question everything I thought I knew about him. He's so different, or is he?

Remembering his first kiss and how badly it rocked me. I wouldn't admit it was lightning—striking. He wasn't the man I wanted to fall for. He was arrogant, and such an asshole, but my toes did curl. And just now, when his lips touched mine, I was swept away, levitating, lost in him.

But, I sigh as I take more pictures of him, desire isn't love. Love is the commitment to honesty.

I lower my phone and stare at him. When he realized he had wronged me, he was truly sorry. And he was truthful about it. He may not be the man I thought I would fall in love with, but I have to see if there's a possibility for happiness with him. Lightning only strikes once, after all, and I would hate to miss out on a lifetime's worth of joy together. There is potential there. And if he's not the one, then at least I tried and lived.

I look up at the sky and say, "Okay, Mom. I'll allow myself a chance to fall in love. I'll try. I'll take a chance on Jocko, and hopefully, the journey leads to a life full of love."

It isn't long before the rescuers are ready to return. Jocko and Lucifer ride on the back of the mule with the sheriff and me., Several times during the trip, I feel Jocko tug my hair. The first time, I ignore him. But the next time is harder, and when I glance back, unsure if it was on purpose, the twinkle in his eyes says it was, and I see the old Jocko again.

Confused, I frown at him, but then he winks, and I realize he's only wanting my attention. He isn't being mean on purpose. I smile, trying to accept him for who he is. I have to open myself up to him and trust him.

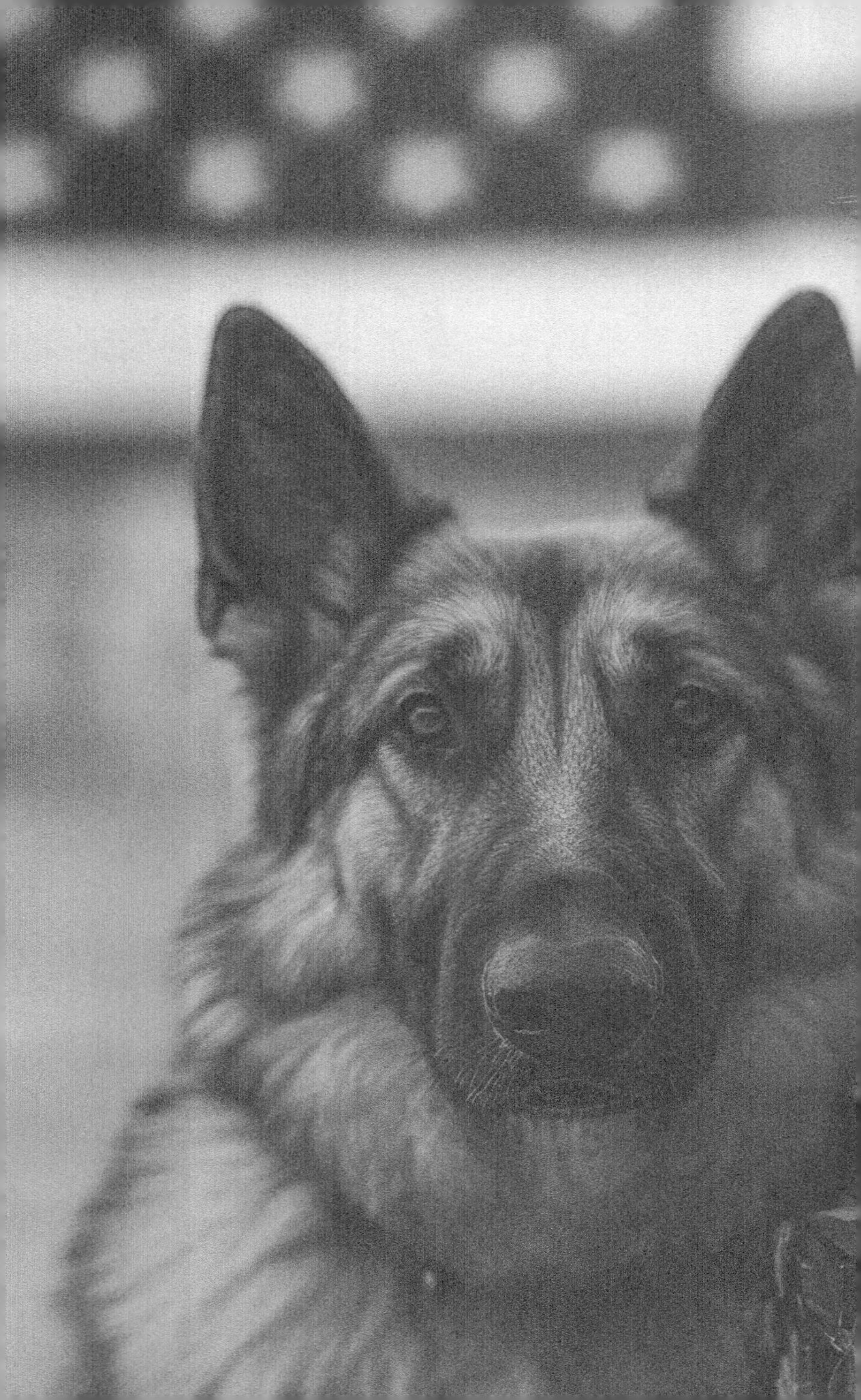

8

Jocko

When we return to the old man's house, Seth is sitting in his Live Oak police cruiser waiting on us. He gets out, waves, then comes over as I shake hands with the family wanting to thank me. I make sure Lucifer gets the credit.

However, Jorja heads straight for Seth's car, opens the passenger door, and gets in.

"Congrats, Cuz." He slaps me on the back as we walk to his car. "Mom has your Welcome Home, Rescue Celebration Combo dinner waiting, and Jorja is to join us."

"Hmm, I'm not so sure that is a good idea."

"Why not?" He looks at her, sitting in the front seat, staring at us. "What did you do to get her panties in a wad?"

I smirk and shrug. "I kissed her."

He laughs out loud. "In that case, bringing Jorja to the dinner is absolutely a good idea."

I cut my eyes at him, and he grins. "Trust me. Taking her home with that look on her face is a rookie mistake. She doesn't need to be alone while she processes what the hell just happened. She needs to be around your family. It's hard to stay pissed off with the Monroes because everyone else will be laughing."

"You are beginning to sound a lot like Uncle John."

He laughs out loud. "I guess there is truth in that old saying, 'The apple doesn't fall far from the tree.'"

The ride back to Live Oak is quiet. Jorja stares out the window. Lost in thought. I stretch and lean my head against the door. Lucifer lays out on the seat and uses me as a pillow. I have no idea what she is thinking, but I hope it's about how mind-blowing our sex is going to be if our kisses are always that earth-shattering because that's what I'm thinking about.

"Hey, Sleepy Head." Seth says, looking in the rearview mirror.

"Yeah, I'm awake."

"We are about five minutes out."

"Okay." I stretch and sit up. Lucifer lifts his head but goes right back to sleep.

Seth keys the radio. "Liz, we are back in town. Heading to Mom's for dinner."

"Roger that. Tell Jocko welcome home and not to be a stranger. I expect him to stop by and see me."

Our eyes meet again and he grins. The sultry undertones of Liz's message aren't lost on either one of us.

"Roger that." He answers.

Jorja turns to him and opens her mouth, but he cuts her off before she can say anything. "I have strict orders, and I'm not about to get on my wife's or my mom's bad side, so don't even go there. I'm delivering the goods as instructed. Everyone wants to know what happened tonight."

She cuts her eyes at me. "It's Jocko's story to tell."

Seth gives her a severe smirk. "Jocko's version will be. Lucifer tracked him. I rescued him. Greg took him to the hospital. The end. Let's eat."

She laughs despite herself.

Jorja

When we arrive, Betty greets us at the door. "Jorja, thank you for coming. It's good to see you. Jocko, we are waiting for Sandy and Greg before we eat, but I have hors d' oeuvres set outside on the deck along with a cooler full of beer. Show Jorja the way, please. Seth, Emmy needs you on Daddy duty. Wendy wants to be held. Lucifer, come here, boy. I have a big bone for you in the kitchen. You can eat it in there, so Pepper can't get it."

Jocko puts his hand on my back, and my skin tingles. The entire way home, all I could think about was his touch. How he's always been the only one that made me feel this way. His goodbye kiss was the kiss of death as far as my love life went. Not only because none of the boys in school were willing to take the risk, but because his kiss ruined it for me. No other man could match it. It was easy, not dating.

God ... smelling the sweetness of his breath as his lips hovered nearly made me swoon. Then the thrill that shot through me when I tasted him again? My needy clit's still throbbing.

As I pass the kitchen, I catch a glimpse of Emmy with an apron on with Wendy on her hip. Bradley's behind Diane with his arms wrapped around her, kissing her cheek, and making faces at Wendy, trying to get her to smile, but her little lips are puckered tight in a mean-face, grumpy scowl.

Jocko stops long enough to poke his head in to say, "Hi, we'll be out back with the beer." They all laugh and tease him about being spoiled rotten.

As soon as we step outside, the quiet of the night hits us. Jocko walks over to the cooler, opens it, and asks, "Do you drink beer?"

I stop and look at him. The question is simple, but it shouts 'you know nothing about each other!' I sigh, "Yes, I drink beer."

"Good." He pulls two bottles out, opens them, and walks over to stand in front of me. He stares into my eyes. I wish I knew what he's thinking, but I'm clueless. I don't know anything about men, and even less about this man. He grins as he offers me a beer.

I sigh and take it. But what I do know is, he isn't the asshole I thought he was. He's a good guy. Actually, he's more than a good guy. He's a hero. He proved it today.

He clinks our bottles. "Here's to a successful day."

"I'll drink to that." I take a big swig wanting to calm my nerves and my emotions that are all over the damn place.

"Hungry? I'm starving." He hands his beer to me to hold, strolls over to the table, gets a plate, fills it full of a little of everything, and walks back to me.

"My God, are you going to eat all that?"

He chuckles. "*We* are going to eat all this. What will you have?"

I try to hand his beer back, but he refuses it. "Pick."

"The cheese sticks look good."

He grins, "Good choice. Easy finger food." He picks it up and holds it out for me to bite.

My heart flip-flops. So much for hanging out as two 'friends' sharing a beer, getting to know each other. He's making the moment intimate. He's going to feed me. Of course, he is. Lovers feed each other finger food, and he's been thinking of us in that way for the last six years. My clit thumps her happiness.

He towers over me, smirking. "Open that beautiful mouth of yours. I'm going to fill it."

God, the man oozes sex appeal! My pussy floods itself. I look away, getting my head in the game, then I look up at him from under my lashes, lick my lips, and open my mouth, waiting for him to insert it.

His eyes hood as his sexy grin spreads across those delicious sculpted lips. Then he slowly inserts the cheese stick inside my mouth.

As soon as my tongue tastes it, my mouth waters and the look on his face changes to need. My breath vanishes with the sensualness of his expression, and my skin flushes.

"Your tongue's very wet, Juicy."

I gently bite down on the cheese stick, not wanting to chomp it in two. That would be ... cruel.

He whispers, "Easy now."

Stopping midway through, my drool pooling, he pulls the stub away, stretching the melted middle between us. All the while, that fucking grin teases me as his dreamy eyes mesmerize mine, hinting at the foreplay to come.

Without breaking eye contact, he sets the plate on the handrail and closes the gap between us. My nipples harden, elongating, desiring his touch. When he lifts his end of the cheese stick, forcing my head all the way back, the hard tips brush his pecs, and the thrill that shoots through me makes my knees weak.

"Open wider, Babe." He hums, and neither of us are thinking about the cheese stick.

God, this man! Willingly, I do as I'm told. Remembering the girth of his boner, I open my mouth wider, and he lowers the string in. By the time his fingers reach my lips, my panties are soaked through again, and my clit is demanding I take care of her soon. I stick my tongue out and lick the stub from between his fingers.

"Hhhhhh," escapes his throat in the sexiest moan I've ever heard. He hovers, watching my mouth working the food, then he whispers. "You're so damn delicious."

My eyes twinkle as I chew, enjoying the power I have over him at the moment. When I swallow, he says, "You and I are going to have a lot of fun together, Juicy." Then he pecks my mouth. The little kiss is extremely satisfying in its promise that later we'll indulge ourselves, but also in that he's committed to us. My heart melts, and I'm content for the moment.

He reaches for the plate, picks it up, and says, "pick for me."

I take another swig on my beer, then examine the goodies. "Men love bacon, so the bacon-wrapped thingie."

He grins. "Men do love bacon." He leans over the plate and maneuvers it with his lips and tongue into his mouth.

I smirk, "You're making that look damn, delicious, Mr. Monroe."

He winks as he chews, then after he swallows, he quickly says, "Beer."

"Hot?" I laugh, then lift his beer to his lips. But he is so tall; the angle is wrong. Trying to help, he leans over, but he only makes it worse. Tipping it too high, I nearly drown him. Laughing out loud at how ridiculous this simple thing has become, I admit. "Oh my god. I totally suck at this."

Slurping the bottle like a pig, he manages to drink most of the beer, and only a small amount trickles down his chin. When he stands back up, he wipes his mouth on his sleeve.

"I'm so sorry!" I laugh. "I wasn't trying to drown you, I promise!"

He chuckles. "Good thing I'm adept at surviving waterboarding."

My face freezes, and all I can do is stare at him. "... waterboarding?"

The term jolts me, and suddenly I see him as a Navy SEAL and know being a SEAL, means there is no doubt that he's killed before.

I raise my hand to my face, mortified. Hiding behind my beer, I shake my head. "Oh my god, Jocko. I can't..."

He sets the plate down, grabs my shoulders, and leans down to look me in the eye. "Hey."

"I can't imagine what you've seen and done."

He takes the beer out of my hand and sets it down by the plate. "Jorja, don't. Don't go there."

"You're a fucking Navy SEAL."

He takes his beer out of my other hand and sets it down next to my beer. Then he takes my hands in his and squats to look directly into my eyes. Then he commands. "Look at me."

When I do, he says, "Look into my eyes."

I stare into his. "What do you see?"

I search them before I answer. "I see ... honor."

He smiles, and my panic eases. "We call what you're feeling 'shock and Awe.'"

I smile weakly back. "That sounds about right."

He says in earnest. "I will always be a SEAL, but I'm a former Navy SEAL. Do you understand what I mean by that?"

I nod, losing myself in his eyes. "I do."

He wraps his arms around me, and I place my face on his chest. Listening to his heartbeat, he says, "I'm just a man, Jorja."

Feeling better, secure in his arms, I smirk. "You're more than just a man, Jocko Monroe." I lean back to look up into his handsome face. "You're a badass!"

He smirks as he tilts his head in agreement.

Just then, we hear a loud commotion in the house. It sounds like something wild is on the loose. Then the back-door bursts open, and Lance, Greg and Sandy's son rushes out, yelling, "Jocko! You're back!" He takes five steps, and he leaps into the air.

Jocko catches him, lifts him overhead, and shakes his body like he is a rag doll.

Lance squeals and giggles.

Jocko tosses him up into the air, pretends to drop him, then pulls him into a sumo wrestler hug, dangling his feet. Then Jocko begins tickling him without mercy.

Lance starts screaming with laughter.

"Quit! Quit! Okay. Okay. I give. I give."

Jocko sets him on his feet, pulls him tight against his chest, and gives him a sincere hug. "Hey, little buddy. How you been?"

He answers, muffled against Jocko's chest. "Good. I've missed you."

"Yeah, it's been a while. You were this big last time I saw you." Jocko holds his hand down around his waist. "You're growing up way too fast."

Lance looks up at him and brags. "I'm eleven and a half!" Then he asks, "Where's your dog?"

"He's inside with Aunt Betty."

"Can I pet him?"

"Sure, just don't try to take his bone away."

Lance rushes back inside. Jocko stares at the closed door for a few moments, and I realize he choked-up holding Lance.

I offer him the plate of food. He takes a cheese stick and pops it in his mouth. Then strolls over to the cooler to get another beer. When he opens the lid, he looks at me. "Are you ready for another?"

"No. I'm still good."

He drops the lid and twists the cap off. "Lightweight."

"I prefer cheap date."

He laughs out loud. "I prefer that too, actually."

We stand together in silence. He eats completely unself-conscious at how much food he puts away, and I enjoy watching him indulge. The way his lips part when the food approaches; the way his tongue touches it, then draws it inside; the movement of his mouth as he chews; the pulsating of his Adam apple as he drains his beer.

Damn. This man does it for me like no one else.

"I'll get you another." I offer as I finish my beer and walk to the cooler. Lifting the lid, I take two out. Then hold them for him to open. He twists the tops off, takes his, clinks the necks, and we both drink, enjoying the comfortable silence between us.

After a minute, I offer, "You know, a good old fashion head noogie is a good transition when Lance is too big for tickling."

He looks at me with that intense stare, and my heart melts.

I'm the luckiest girl alive.

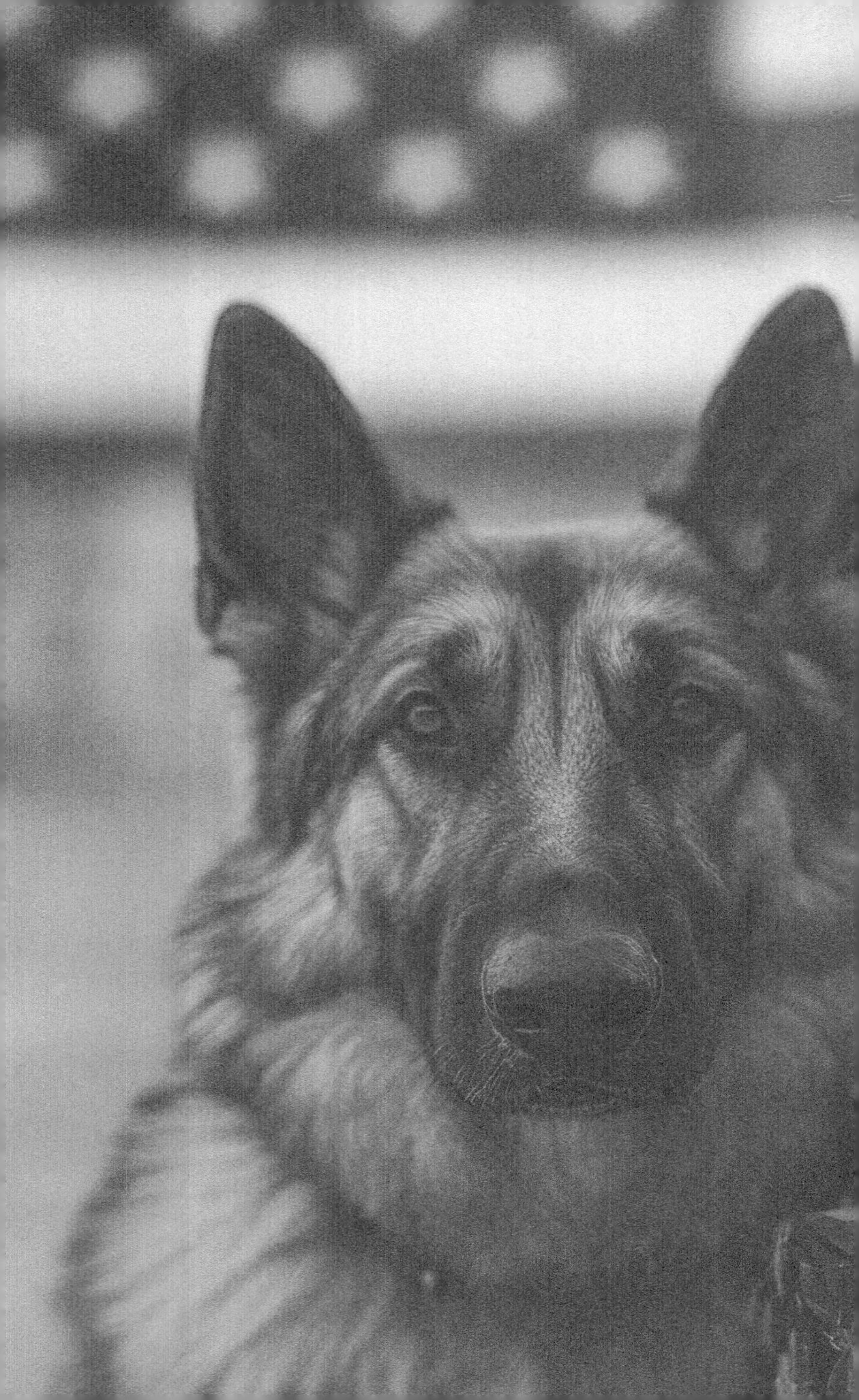

9

Jorja

Sitting around the table, eating dinner, Jocko and the three Monroe brothers throw barbs at each other while everyone is laughing their asses off. I've never experienced this sort of family dynamic before, having been raised by a single mom. Some of the things they say to each other make me cringe, but those are the very things that they laugh the hardest at.

Guy humor is so different from girl humor. I can see now that back in high school, Jocko was teasing me. I just didn't understand that.

Occasionally, John chimes in, and everyone roars when he does.

Bradley and Seth are just beginning their story about how they entered Greg's name in *Southern Family Magazine's* Hot Dad Contest without him knowing it when Lance throws both hands in the air and stands up. "May I be excused?"

Greg looks at him. "NO! Sit down!"

Everyone howls.

Lance looks right at Sandy. "Mom, please?"

She nods as the story takes off.

Lance scoots his chair back to leave, and Jocko waves him over. When he arrives, Jocko leans back in his chair, turns slightly toward me, and puts his arm around Lance. Lance rests his hand on his shoulder as Jocko says, "Hey, buddy, do me a favor. Take Luce outside with you."

Lance's face lights up, and he spins around. "Come on, Luce. Let's go play outside with Pepper."

Jocko watches Lance and Lucifer leave, then turns back to the table and trades barbs with the three brothers.

Occasionally, Jocko glances at me to make sure I'm enjoying myself. Which is really sweet since I have nothing to contribute to the conversation, but I'm really enjoying watching him in the family dynamic. The Monroes are tight, and I gain real insight into who he is as a non-military man.

When the dessert is passed around, I take a piece of Betty's homemade cherry pie, top it with a scoop of vanilla ice cream, and eat about half, then push the remaining over to Jocko. He sees it and looks at me. "You are welcome to my cherry pie."

The expression that falls over his face says, finishing off food equates to the same intimacy level as the feeding of food as far as relationships go, and my tummy flip-flops. I lift my eyebrows as I smile, confirming we have leapfrogged a lot of levels in only a few hours.

He slides my plate over, stacks it on top of his, then

scoops a big bite. As it travels to his lips, his eyes tease me. *He intends to eat more than my piece of Betty's cherry pie.*

I blush. *Sex is imminent.*

After the dinner dishes are done, Betty takes her apron off. "Let's all go out to the backyard so Jorja can share what she witnessed today."

Everyone files out of the house and finds a place to listen. Betty, John, Seth, and Emmy walk over to the lounge chairs. Emmy's cradling Wendy, who's fallen asleep, but Betty holds her arms out for her granddaughter, and Emmy places her little girl gently in her arms. Bradley and Diane sit on the edge of the porch, holding hands. While Greg and Sandy stretch out on the grass with Lance, Pepper, and Lucifer.

Jocko tries to join them, but I grab his hand and pull him up on the deck with me. "Oh, no, you don't. You're the main attraction."

Everyone laughs.

When I clear my throat to begin, Sandy pipes up. "Give us all the details, Jorja. Don't leave anything out."

"Of course!" I grin, and Jocko rolls his eyes and moans.

Everyone laughs again.

Looking over at Greg and Sandy, I begin. "First, let me say it was an honor to be a part of the rescue. Thank you for including me."

They share a quick look. Sandy gives Greg a smug smile.

I begin my accounting of the rescue with, "After we landed, and Jocko met with the rescue team ...." I share with them how watching Jocko care for Lucifer as he removed his eye goggles and other gear and the way Lucifer focused on Jocko with total trust made me realize they share a profound bond. Then I describe how Jocko addressed the rescue team volunteers, rallying them to the task but not mincing his words, telling them "to stay 'the bleep' out of the way."

Everyone chuckles, including Jocko, and he shrugs.

"Once Lucifer sniffed the old man's shirt and had his scent, Jocko gave the command to track and followed his own advice. He got 'the bleep' out of Lucifer's way."

Everyone chuckles again.

"The way Jocko allowed Lucifer to work independently of commands impressed the heck out of me. He totally trusted Lucifer to do his job and find Mr. Romano."

"Once Lucifer put his nose to the ground, we were off. They sprinted across the field Greg landed the helicopter in, then blindly charged into the woods."

Looking around, giving them all eye contact, I describe how the 'dynamic duo' navigated the rough terrain and dodged trees, all while hauling ass.

"Then ... they stopped."

I pause to let the tension build.

"When we pulled up next to them in the mule, the sheriff asked if they had lost the scent."

Holding my hands to each side of my mouth, I lean toward them. "I think Jocko was a little insulted the man doubted them."

Everyone chuckles, and when I look at Jocko, he gives me a killer head nod.

Lance asks, "What happened? Why did they stop?"

"They needed a water break. They had been running cross-country for twenty minutes at a brutal pace. I asked the sheriff how far we had come, and he estimated two, maybe two and a half miles."

Jocko raises an eyebrow and shakes his head, and I laugh.

"Yes, he miscalculated. Sitting in the cruiser waiting for you and Seth, I calculated the distance and the speed. From Mr. Romano's house to where we found him was four miles. The time tracking was right at 22 minutes. That means Jocko and Lucifer were going approximately 11 miles an hour through the woods. At that pace, they were covering a mile every five and a half minutes."

Bradley whistles and Jocko gives me a sexy pleased smirk.

Seth pipes up. "He ran a four, seven, 40-yard dash in high school. That's still the fastest time, by the way."

Lance asks, "How fast is that?"

"That is right at seventeen miles per hour."

"Wow! How fast can Lucifer run?"

Jocko tells him, "He's been clocked at thirty-five miles per hour."

"WOW!"

Seth puts it in perspective for Lance. "He runs faster than the speed limit in town."

Lance pats Lucifer. "Dang, boy! You're fast!"

"He's got twice as many legs," Greg adds.

Betty says, "Back to the story, please. It's past my bedtime."

Everyone laughs.

"We weren't on the trail again two minutes before Jocko, and Lucifer take off at a dead run. Then Jocko shouts 'STAY', and Lucifer locks up. But Jocko doesn't. He barrels past, plants a foot, and...." I demonstrate the motion of his arms lifting over his head, then bring them back to my chest. "He dove off the riverbank! My heart almost stopped beating."

I look at Jocko. "The minute it took for us to arrive in the mule, get out, get to the edge, and spot you swimming, has got to be the longest minute of my life."

I tell his family without waiting to see how my words affected him. "He was swimming across the current. Mr. Romano was holding on to a fallen tree in the middle of the river."

Betty gasps.

"How Mr. Romano got there is for the investigators to figure out, but he would've surely drowned if Jocko hadn't swum out and saved him."

Jocko clears his throat.

I tilt my head and turn back around to look at him. "By the way, what did you say to him when you got there? He was laughing so hard."

Jocko's eyes twinkle, "I asked to see his fishing license."

Everyone laughs.

I turn back to the family. "By this time, Greg is hovering overhead. A couple of deputies have waded out to stabilize the rescue basket while Jocko swims back with Mr. Romano. They strap him in, then hoist him up to the helicopter. And he waves like he's in a parade, happy as a lark." I show them, "Of course, we all waved back."

Everyone laughs again.

I walk over to look Jocko in the eye. "I want you to know witnessing the way you selflessly saved that man's life was the most moving experience I have ever had."

His eyes bore into mine, and the look on his face is the same one that has haunted my nights for the past six years. I smile at him, happy I know what that look means now.

It means everything.

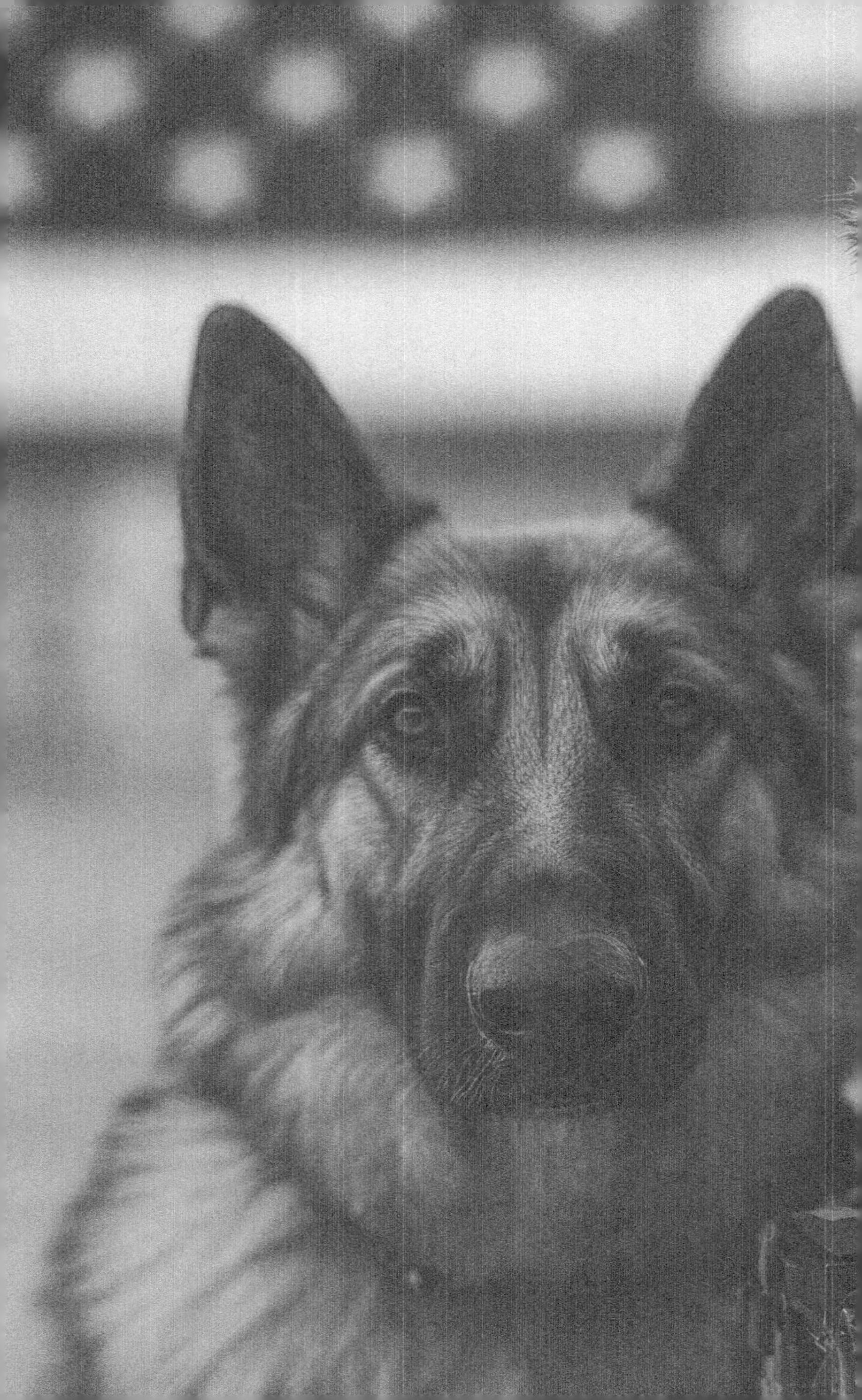

10

Jocko

Jorja's laughing as her phone is passed around. She narrates what's happening at the time the video was shot. "Lucifer was so excited when he heard Jocko coming back. His whole body was wiggling, but he stayed right there until Jocko called him." She glances at me, and our eyes lock. For a second, my world stops spinning. Her look says, 'I'm your girl.' Then she's laughing with Lance and agreeing Lucifer has 'happy feet.'

I pull my phone out to check the time. It is 9:30. If the party hasn't broken up by 10:00, I'm faking fatigue.

Uncle John brings a beer. "The world has righted itself, hasn't it?"

"Yes, sir. It has."

"I trust you won't let her off the hook."

"I don't intend to."

"Good. I'll leave you to it, but if you run into a situation where you need advice, don't hesitate to ask."

I take a draw on the beer. "I appreciate that. I'm formulating my rules of engagement now."

He claps me on the back. "Don't take no for an answer."

"I won't."

Aunt Betty joins us, sliding her arm around my waist. "It's good to have you home, Jocko."

"Yes, ma'am. It's good to be home. Thank you for dinner."

She squeezes my waist. "Just tell me it was delicious."

Uncle John and I chuckle. "It was delicious. Better than I remember."

She smiles, then nods toward Jorja. "That sweet girl didn't date after you left."

I smile, looking at Jorja. Her hair floats as she talks with her hands. "I know."

"Your goodbye was the talk of the town for months."

Uncle John scolds her. "Betty, the boy hasn't been home a week. Don't start in on him."

She cuts her eyes at Uncle John, then tells me as she rubs my back, "You pick up right where you left off. She's been waiting for you."

Uncle John takes her shoulders, steering her away, giving her down the road about my not needing her matchmaking skills.

Greg and Sandy walk over. He holds out my truck keys. "We brought your truck from the airport."

"Thanks." I take them and stuff them in my pocket.

"I was just telling Greg that now he knows why I picked Jorja to tell your story for the magazine. She has a way with words that make a story come alive. She's a talented writer."

Greg defends himself. "I accused her of setting you two up when she asked if they could go on the rescue."

"Ah.... Well, thanks for assigning her regardless of the reason."

She smiles. "You're welcome. It's nice to finally meet you. I've heard some wi... wonderful things about you."

I laugh. "I bet you heard some wild things too."

"Some raised the hair on my head."

Greg butts in. "Listen, cuz, we need a favor."

"Sure, anything."

"Lance's spending the night here tonight because Sandy and me...." She elbows him. "Oomph."

Then she takes over the sentence. "Had a date planned."

Greg continues where he was before the elbow. "... are making mom another grand-baby."

She smiles as if he hasn't said a word.

I take a long draw on my beer, enjoying the hell out of their playful love.

She, very professionally, asks. "Would you mind seeing that Jorja gets home safely?"

I look over at Jorja. She's taking a beer from Diane, then they're laughing. I smirk and look back at Sandy. "Go. I got Jorja."

She slips her hand in Greg's. "Come on, Make Me Moan Monroe."

He looks back at me with a grin as they sneak out unnoticed through the gate in the fence.

Bradley walks over to Diane and Jorja, then leans over to watch the video. They all laugh, and Jorja cuts her eyes at me. I toast her with my beer, and she smiles, then excuses herself and heads over.

Watching her walk to me, happy, I marvel at the perfect way our reunion's gone down. Of all the hundreds of different scenarios I played out in my mind, a rescue wasn't one of them.

Emmy says behind me. "Seth tells me you would like to continue jumping."

I turn to her voice and nod as she steps beside me. "That's right."

She laughs as Jorja arrives. "It gets in your blood."

"Yes, it does."

"What gets in your blood?" Jorja asks.

"Free-falling," I answer.

She gives us a look that clearly says we've lost our fucking minds, and Emmy quickly counters with, "I prefer skydiving or parachute jumping."

Jorja tilts her head, unconvinced. "It doesn't matter what label you put on it. It's still too dangerous for me."

Remembering her terror in the helicopter, I poke her. "Jorja is truly terrified of flying."

She sticks her tongue out at me.

Needing as much as wanting to feel her body against mine, I take the bait, lunging for her. Squealing, she thinks about fleeing, but my arms wrap around her before she can take a single step.

Laughing, she thrashes, trying to get away. Her softness and scent pummel my senses, and my balls draw up, preparing for more. *Mmmm, this is a bad idea in gym clothes.* I shift her to a headlock and practice a little noogie love on her peanut.

She squeals giggling, "Emmy, help me!"

Emmy laughs, "Oh, hell no. You're on your own."

"Ahhhhh."

When I release her, I pull her uptight and press her curves into my body. She feels perfect there. Leaving my arm draped over her shoulders, I ask Emmy, "What were we talking about?"

Emmy beams at us as one of Jorja's hand slips inside my T-shirt, tickling the arch on my back as she slides it around to rest on my hip, and her other hand rests on my abs.

"I was about to ask if you would like to participate in the exhibition jump on the Fourth of July?"

"Can I blow red, white, and blue smoke?"

"Absolutely!"

"Count us in then."

Jorja panics, "Us?"

Laughing, I look down into her big eyes. "Me and Luce, Babe."

"Oh my god. That would be fabulous!" Emmy says as Jorja presses her hand into my abs and strokes me in a slow, sexy circle, keeping the cum load in my balls.

Bradley and Diane walk up. "What would be fabulous?"

Emmy turns her smile on them. "Jocko and Lucifer are going to jump at the exhibition with red, white, and blue smoke."

Bradley grins, "Show-off!"

I give him a head nod as Emmy asks Diane, "Now, all I need is someone to sing the National Anthem."

"I would love to." Diane agrees as Aunt Betty and Seth walk up.

"Would love to what, dear?"

"Sing the National Anthem at the Fourth of July exhibition."

"Ah. Good." She tells Emmy.

Seth reaches for Emmy's hand. "Wendy's asleep." He looks at us and announces, "We're going to get out of here. Jocko, congrats again on a successful rescue." He holds out his hand.

"Thanks for the call. It felt good to work again and was rewarding to be able to help." I lean toward him to shake it. Jorja's hands move, and I squeeze her shoulder, trying to keep her in place. But then Emmy reaches for a hug, and Jorja retreats.

"Welcome home, and congrats. I'll be in touch about jumping."

"I'll stop by Wings Away tomorrow."

"Perfect."

Seth takes her hand and heads to the gate in the fence. Bradley steps up with his hand outstretched too, and he and Diane repeat what was said by the others for the most part. In-between saying goodbye to Seth and Diane, I look over at Jorja.

She's realized I'm taking her home.

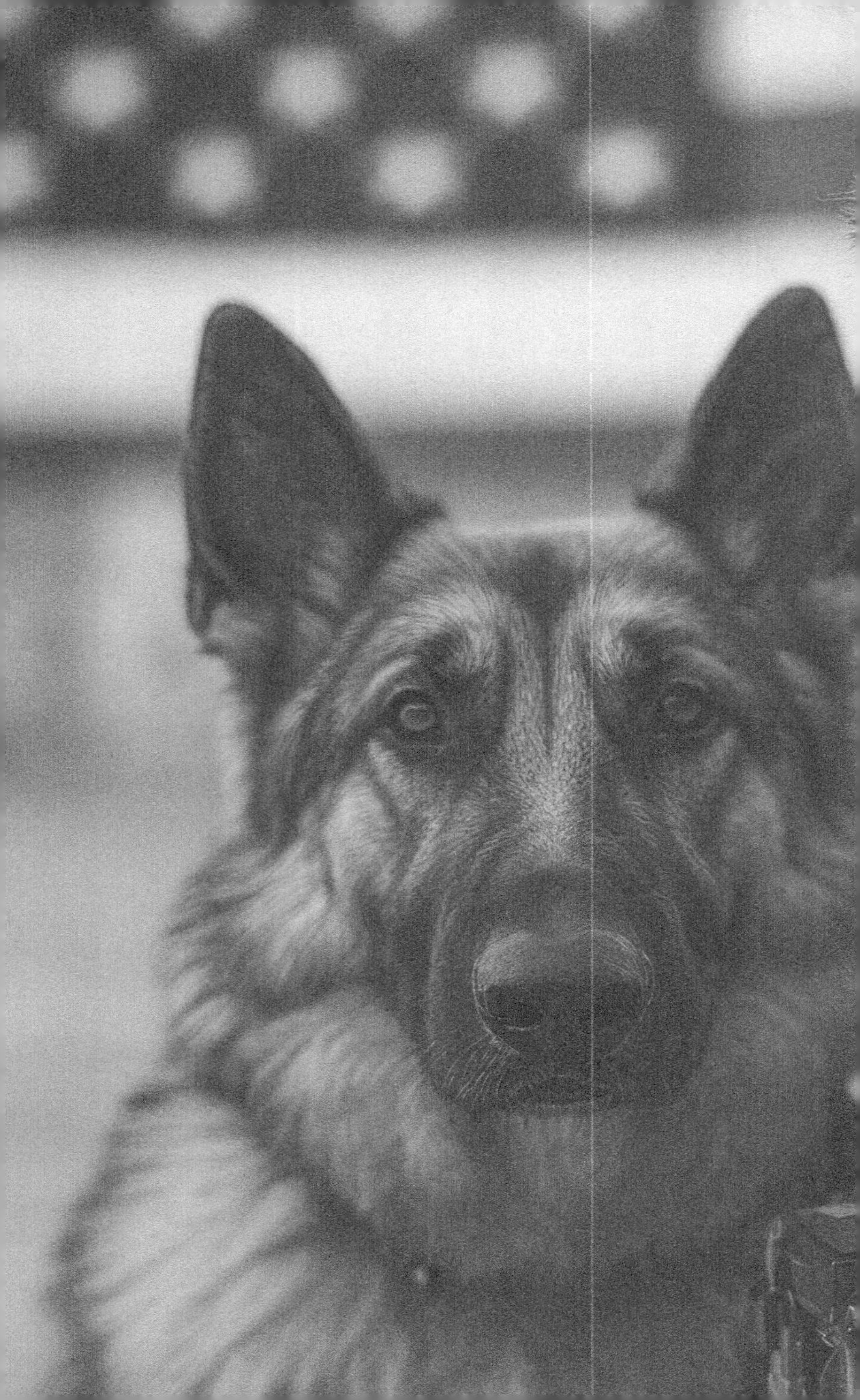

11

Jorja

———

As Bradley and Diane walk away, Lance runs up with Lucifer and Pepper.

"Can Lucifer spend the night?"

Jocko takes a knee to discuss it man to man. "Not this time. He's still adjusting to civilian life."

Lance's hopeful face drops.

"When he's ready for a dog sitter, you'll be the one I call. In the meantime, you need to come over and learn his commands. He has had extensive training, so he needs someone who understands him."

Lance nods as he looks longingly at Lucifer.

Jocko says, "He has some amazing tricks. Want to see some?"

Lance's face lights up again. "Now?"

"Sure. Go grab a balloon." He stands and watches Lance run off. The love on his face shines like a beacon, and my heart melts a little more. He isn't the meanie I always thought he was.

"Is everything okay, dear?" Betty puts her arm around me and gives me a gentle squeeze. "I take it his arrival surprised you too?"

I nod my head.

"Overwhelmed?"

"Yes, ma'am. Jocko called it 'shock and awe.'"

She smiles. "From the day Jocko was born, he has been a force to be reckoned with."

We look at him standing tall, proud, confident, and relaxed, waiting for Lance to return with the balloon.

God, he is sexy as hell.

Betty continues softly, "But after his parents died, even more so."

I cut my eyes at her, and her face softens when she looks at him. "Did you know his father was John's brother?"

I shake my head.

"And his mother was one of my best friends? When they passed in that horrific accident, we took him in. We were worried Jocko's emotional scars would be his undoing. He couldn't talk about it. He bottled it all up inside. My boys stepped up and made sure he knew they were there if he needed them, but it was Lance that pulled him through it."

I look back at him, seeing him through her eyes. Watching him as he takes a balloon from Lance, then bats it straight up in the air.

As it returns, Lucifer leaps twelve feet to bat it back up.

Lance shouts, "WOW!"

Betty continues, "We couldn't be more proud of the man he's become."

We watch in silence, then suddenly, I confess the thing

that has bothered me the most. "I didn't heard at all from him the whole time he was gone."

Betty squeezes my shoulder again. "I know that hurt, and I won't make excuses for why I think he didn't, but I'll tell you this. He asked about you every time he called to check-in."

I look at her and she smiles, "He always asked how you were doing when he called. He didn't ask for details, just that you were okay."

The balloon floats down toward us, so I step forward and bat it into the air. Lucifer leaps, and his teeth pop it.

Lance's "Ahhhhh" makes everyone laugh.

Jocko ruffles Lucifer's fur as he gently explains to Lance that his 'fur missile' needs to eat and get to bed.

I turn to Betty and hug her. "Thank you."

She smiles. "No thanks needed."

Jocko

Aunt Betty waves goodbye from the porch. "Now, don't you be a stranger, Jocko. You hear me?"

I throw up my hand, turn around to face her, and walk backward, saying, "Just let me know when the cornbread is cooking."

She laughs and goes inside.

On the ride to Jorja's car, she's quiet, staring out the window. "Hey, you okay?"

"Yeah, just tired."

Pulling up to the driver's side of her car, I put my truck

in park and then turn to face her. She unbuckles her seatbelt and looks at me. "If anyone had told me yesterday, what I would do today, I would never have believed them."

"Still in shock and awe?"

"Will it go away one day?"

"God, I hope not." I grin at her.

She laughs. "I assume you know I'm writing an article on you for *Southern Family Magazine*."

"Yeah, Sandy called earlier to ask if I was cool with it. Honestly, the only reason I am is because you are writing it."

She smiles, "I need your digits."

I grin. "Yes, you do!"

She pulls her phone and enters my number. Then she turns and tells Lucifer, "Goodnight, Luce."

She reaches to open her door, and I grab her arm. She hesitates but then opens it and slides out.

A rush of emotions hit me as she slips out of my grasp, and the sound of the truck door closing jars my gut. She walks around in the headlights tucking a wayward strand of hair behind her ear. She has no idea how beautiful she is.

I put my window down as she unlocks her car door. "I'm going to follow you home. I want to make sure you get inside safely."

She opens the door. "That's sweet, but not necessary. You go home and feed the hero."

"Let's do lunch tomorrow."

"I only get 30 minutes."

I smirk. "I like the way 'only 30 minutes' doesn't sound like enough time."

"We have a lot to talk about." She lowers herself into the seat. "Goodnight, Jocko."

She cranks it and waves sweetly to me as she pulls

away. I tail her anyway. When she turns into her drive, I turn in too and kill the lights. Her brakes stay illuminated. I smirk, hoping she's trying to decide sleep or sex.

When she opens her car door, my fingers cross on the steering wheel, and I lean in for a better view. Her sneakers hit the ground, and she stands.

Sex. Sex. Come on, Babe. Choose sex. Sleep is overrated.

She spins around, puts a knee in the seat, and reaches across for something. Her beautiful, bodacious booty tempts the hell out of my self-discipline, and my hand moves to the door latch. *Come on .... Let's do this....*

She backs out, swings a satchel over her shoulder, closes the car door, then turns away.

Dammit. I pop the steering wheel. *Looks like I'll be whacking off one more time.*

She bounces up the porch steps two at a time. Her body pulls a moan out of my mouth. She's had too much shock, but it's all going to be awe from now on.

She unlocks her door, pushes it open, hits the interior lights, then turns to me and waves again as she closes the door.

"Goodnight, Juicy."

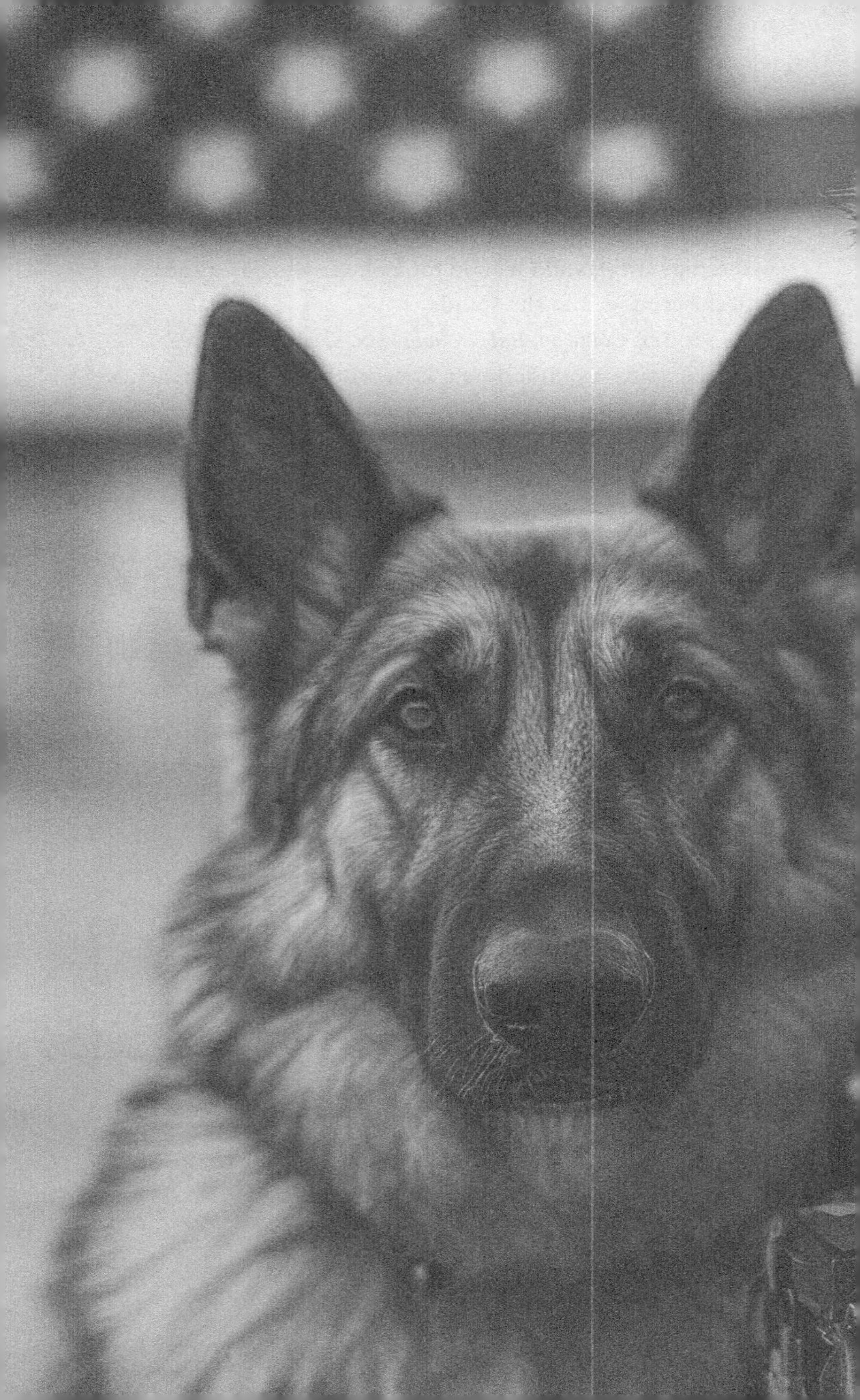

12

Jorja

> Good morning. I would like to start your interview today.

>> GOOD MORNING. ARE YOU AN EARLY BIRD?

> YES. I'M AN EARLY RISER, IF THAT'S WHAT YOU MEAN.

>> GOOD. EARLY BIRDS GET THE WORM, YOU KNOW WHAT I MEAN?

I laugh out loud.

> If you are available, how about lunch?

>> OH, I'M AVAILABLE, BABE. I AM SO AVAILABLE.

I laugh again.

> Can you meet me at Lola's Diner?

>> *I WOULD RATHER PICK YOU UP, TAKE YOU TO GOLD COAST WINERY, AND EAT YOU IN A PRIVATE "TASTING" ROOM.*

My clit awakens with that one.

> I can't commit to longer than half an hour without permission from Sandy. I'll have to let you know.

>> *I'M ONLY A PHONE CALL AWAY.*

When I push open the door at Donut Dilemma, it feels like everyone turns to look, but I know it's just my imagination. Everyone here knew I was the only person in Live Oak that was in the damn dark.

Last night, lying in bed, I processed everything that had been said between Jocko and me from the beginning until now to the best of my recollection. I came to the conclusion that it was simply a case of miscommunication. Which should be easy to remedy.

I check the time on my phone. Twenty minutes before the official workday begins. The line moves, and I step closer to the counter. Macey looks up and sees me in line. She mouths, "Told you so!"

"Yes, you did." I mouth back.

She swipes her current customer's card, hands it back, and delivers her cheesy, cheeky customer care quip. "Thank you for solving your Donut Dilemma with us."

The man drops a tip in her glass jar and leaves with his order.

I step up to the counter. A grin bigger than yesterday's is on her face. "Your usual, boo?"

"Please."

She shouts my order over her shoulder as the man makes his way to a table.

I slide my credit card to her.

"So, spill the beans. What happened?" Her eyes bore into mine.

I begin giving her the low down on the rescue, but she interrupts me as she swipes it.

"Girl! I'm talking about *after* the rescue." She slides it back to me.

"Oh. Well, Betty Monroe ...."

"I want to know how the sex was." She cuts her eyes behind her. "Hurry. Your order's going to be here, and I'll have to wait all day for the details."

"You are unbelievable, you know that?" I pick my card up and drop it in my satchel.

"Oh. My. God. You didn't?" She rolls her eyes. "You're the one that is unbelievable."

She looks over her shoulder and sees Mario putting the top on my coffee. She leans in and whispers. "How do you *not* fuck a man like that brains out the first chance you get?"

We stand glaring at each other as Mario walks up.

"Good morning, Jorja."

"Morning, Mario."

He pushes my order to me, and Macey puts her hand on his arm. "I got this, Mario. Your job is just to deliver the food to the counter."

He nods, "Have a good day, Jorja."

"You too."

I reach for my coffee and cake, but Macey places her hand on mine and squeezes. "Listen, sweetie, you know I love you. You need to either choose Jocko or let him move on! He doesn't deserve to be strung along anymore."

I stare at her, dumbfounded. "I haven't been stringing him along."

"Not intentionally, but you have been." She presses her lips together. "As your bestie, I'm being real with you. You need to fuck the poor man. Today!"

"What?"

"You're always overthinking and analyzing everything. But this time, you need to let your heart tell your head to shut the fuck up." She looks over her shoulder again. No one is paying us any attention. "You're a grown woman. Go ahead. Get down and dirty with him. It will be crystal clear to you then." She releases my hand. "Just fuck him and feel it, then you can stop lying to yourself and admit that you're his girl."

We stare at each other. She gives me the 'eye,' and I stubbornly refuse to receive it.

Another customer steps up to place their order.

I take my food and walk to the door. Right before I push it open, I glance back at her. She mouths, "Today."

The door shuts behind me.

Sitting at my desk, sipping my coffee and fingering my cake, Macey's advice echoes around and around. *"You're always overthinking and analyzing everything. But this time, you need to let your heart tell your head to shut the fuck up."*

I take a bite and a sip, then swirl them around in my mouth. Admitting to yourself that you've been wrong should be easy to do, but I find myself struggling with it.

Was I wrong to feel abandoned and humiliated? Did I feel

that way only because I'm scarred? Because my dad left us? Or would I have felt that way anyway because he didn't say anything? No one else thought he had abandoned me. Why?

If only he had said, "Wait for me." But even if he had, would I have felt any less abandoned?

I try hard to separate my emotions from what happened and analyze them, but I can't.

My phone vibrates, and I flip it over to read the text. It's Macey.

> Get out of your head! Just do him!

The office door opens, and Sandy walks in. "Good morning, Jorja."

"Morning, Sandy."

She tells me as she passes my desk on her way to her office. "I looked over your article on Magnolia's Corner. Good work."

Sandy is a perfectionist, so when she gives a compliment, it means something.

"Thank you."

"When you finish your breakfast," she glances at the clock. It's 7:52. "Come into my office. We need to discuss your new assignment.

At 8;01, I tap lightly on Sandy's office door, then push it open. She's on the phone, looking over some papers on her desk. She waves me in to take a seat.

"Yes, that's fine. Whatever you think is best. Listen, Jorja just walked in. I need to go." She winks at me. "We will be up to see you this weekend. Love you too, Daddy."

She hangs up, shakes her head, and says, "I love him, but...."

"I admire your ability to balance family and business."

"Thanks. It's not easy." She opens her laptop and gets right down to business. "I want you to begin working on the article for the contest immediately while your emotions are still fresh and raw. Your story last night of how you felt having witnessed the rescue was very moving. Rather than an analytical article, I want you to write a testimonial-type piece based on your feelings."

She types while she talks. "I want to come at this on a different level. I want to put the emphasis on the 'among us' part of the phrase. Meaning the men and women we know and love personally, not acquaintances in our communities. Not the collective group. Not the rescue team, but the husband/wife/partner who is a part of the team."

She looks at me to make sure I'm on board. I nod.

"I want the reader to identify with someone they love that goes above and beyond. Let's pull on their heartstrings."

I nod again, and she stops typing and leans forward and looks me dead in the eye. "Your story last night took a man who is larger than life. The epitome of the word hero. And made us see him not as a Navy SEAL but as the man you love."

She looks over at the picture of Greg she has on her desk and continues, "When I looked at my husband, I saw him with the same love and appreciation for who he is and what he does."

She looks back up at me. "That's what I want our readers to feel when they finish your article. I want them to feel the pride and love for their personal hero who's just an everyday dude but who goes above and beyond."

She smiles again. "Can you do that?"

I nod. "I can do that."

"Good. I want the first draft on my desk in two weeks. Don't worry about coming into the office. You can work remotely. Research your subject thoroughly." She smiles, and I blush.

"Yes, ma'am."

As I close the door to her office, I lean against it. She said she could see the love on my face for Jocko.

The office door opens, and Desiree and Britney come in together. I give them a smile and walk to my desk. "I saw Jocko yesterday."

They make a beeline for me "And ...?"

"And ... Wowzer!"

"Did he surprise you?"

I laugh, "Yes, he did. But not how you thought he would."

"Tell us! Please!" Britney begs.

And Desiree threatens, "You better not hold back. We want all the romantic details!"

I laugh and recount for them how this big, massive hunk lifted me into the helicopter and held me tight while I shook with fear during the flight. "I had no idea who he was, but was so thankful for having someone strong to hide my face against."

They both roll their eyes, "You are so freaking lucky!"

I smile, thankful I've finally accepted that fact. "And when we landed, and I went to thank him." I take a deep breath, "My god, y'all." I shake my head. "You can't imagine how I felt with I recognized his mouth and he said, 'Sup, Jorja?'"

Both of them, "Awe!" But Britney asks, "Did he kiss you then?"

I shake my head, "No, there was a man to rescue."

"But he did kiss you?"

I blush, biting my bottom lip, "Oh, hell, yeah! He kissed me, and it was...." I grin at them.

"Everything!" Desiree finishes the sentence for me.

I nod, agreeing. "Yes. It was everything."

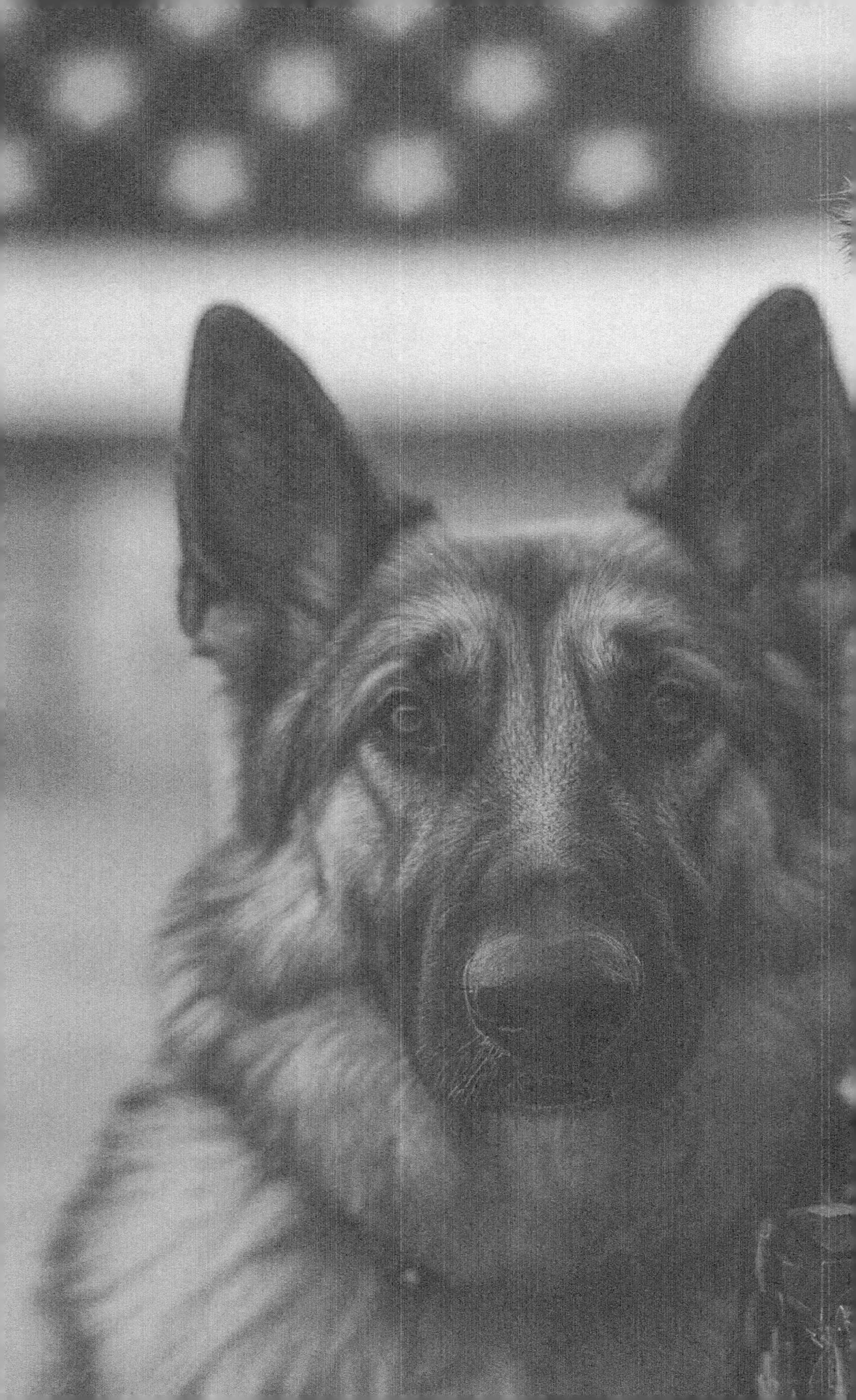

13

Jocko

Sitting in my truck at Wings Away waiting for Emmy to arrive, I keep staring at my phone, waiting for a text from Jorja and rereading the messages from this morning. I was salty after enduring another night alone.

Every time I closed my eyes, I could see her image clear as day and hear her melodic voice echoing in my mind. I could smell her scent on my clothes and taste her sweet kiss on my lips. I tried to whack off, but I no longer need a Jorja-hand-job to keep my sanity. I need to sink the son-of-a-bitch deep inside her to assure her I'm not blowing sunshine up her ass. I mean what I say and say what I mean.

I have gone through hell. I have paid my debt to my country, and it was an honor to do so. But now, I'm ready to focus on my life and my legacy. I'm ready to settle down, get married, have babies. But I learned last night the girl I was hoping to sweep off her feet and make a happily ever after life with has hated me the entire time.

What a mind fuck! What a fucking mind fuck!

Laying there in the dark with a hard-on and blue balls, I focused on the objective and solidified my rules of engagement.

- #1. Deter attacks.
- #2. Neutralize hostility.
- #3. Counteract aversion.
- #4. Take the offensive.
- #5. Peace through superior firepower.

I'll be the victor of her heart, and Juicy Jorja is going to surrender her beautiful spoils to me. I don't care how long it takes. SEALS never quit!

I look at my phone one more time as Emmy pulls up, but nothing.

She waves, and Lucifer and I get out of the truck. He trots around, sniffing, looking for a place to piss while she unlocks the door.

"Good morning. Have you been waiting long?"

"No," I lie.

"Betty called to bring Wendy some...." She laughs. "Never mind. Mommy talk."

"Wendy is a cutie."

"Thanks. She is a handful." She swings the door open. "Come on in."

"Psst." Lucifer looks up and trots over.

Emmy laughs. "He minds better than she does."

"He minds better than most kids do."

"Would you like some coffee?"

"No, thank you. I'm good." I walk around looking at her

pictures hanging on the walls while she brews a pot. "You have got some good candid shots."

"Thanks. Leroy, my jump coordinator, took those." She pours herself a cup of coffee. "So, let's discuss the exhibition."

I follow her into her office to go over the event schedule and the gear I'll need. When we're finished discussing all the jump details, I offer, "Once we're on the ground, would you like to have Lucifer demonstrate some of his K9 skills?"

"Of course! What do you have in mind?"

"That depends on the location, but he handles a mean obstacle course. Makes it look easy."

Her eyes light up. "Like America's Top Dog?"

I shake my head. "I don't know what that is."

"It's a K9 competition on TV. They have to navigate an obstacle course. I'll call Demi and see if she's game to put it together."

I stand. "Well, I'll get out of your hair and let you get to work."

She comes around her desk to walk me out. "This is going to be epic, you know."

"Doesn't America's Birthday deserve epic?"

"That it does."

―――

Heading back into town, my original plan was to stop by Home Depot to purchase the first items to begin the backyard playground for Lucifer, but I change my mind when I check the time. It's 11:00, and I still haven't heard from Jorja. Time to instigate my Rules of Engagement.

Driving past *Southern Family Magazine*, looking for a place to park, I spot her car in the lot. The street is crowded, so I go around the block and find a single parking spot around the corner. I'll have to walk in front of the boutiques to get there, which will probably mean I'll be recognized, and someone will stop me wanting to welcome me home, which could turn a simple two-minute hike into ten minutes or more. But, if I have a bouquet from Magnolia's Corner, it'll be obvious I'm on a mission, and I'll score some major points with Jorja. All girls love flowers.

With Lucifer heeling, I buy a beautiful bouquet of red, yellow, and purple wildflowers, and the people I pass on the street simply say, "Welcome home, Jocko."

When I enter the magazine's front office, I tell the grinning receptionist. "I have this very special delivery for Jorja Jones."

She nods and points me to the correct office.

When I pull open the door, I see a spacious area with ten desks. Several are face to face, while the others sit alone. The room buzzes with activity, and no one notices me. I spot Jorja typing on her laptop with earbuds in. Her hair's pulled into a curly ponytail. She's wearing a white buttoned collared shirt with the top two buttons undone. The fabric sags, gaping open and exposing a full view of her ample cleavage. Immediately, my balls draw up and start to fill. She looks every bit the sassy, sexy secretary men drool over in their dreams.

When I enter the room, I take two steps to the side and signal Lucifer to stay. I'm spotted by a girl in the back that looks vaguely familiar. She freezes, and her mouth drops open. I put my finger to my lips and silently 'shush' her. She nods, but her hand waves frantically for the girl next to her to pay attention.

By the time I'm standing in front of Jorja's desk with the flowers hidden behind my back, she's the only one unaware

I'm there. Even Sandy's opened her door to watch. I give her a head nod, and she laughs.

I slowly start pushing Jorja's laptop closed.

Her face flashes a frown. She's annoyed. When she looks up to discover who the fuck is fucking with her, I notice she's wearing dark brown eyeshadow with black eyeliner and dark red lipstick.

Goddamn, she is drop-dead gorgeous! Thank God I wore tight briefs today. Otherwise, the dragon wouldn't be invisible.

Her expression changes instantly. Her mouth falls open. "Sup, Juicy?"

Then back again to annoyed because ... that name. She cuts her eyes to see if anyone overheard, and I smile at her sheepishly as I pull the flowers out from behind my back.

"This is me...." I lift my eyebrows. "You know."

She smiles as "aahs" fill the room. Then she removes her earbuds and stands to take them.

Fuck me. Her white shirt is tucked into a red pencil skirt. Her hourglass curves accentuated perfectly. Her heels must be high because her tits and ass are posed superbly.

"They're beautiful. Thank you." She sticks her nose into them and sniffs.

"You're welcome. Are we doing lunch today?"

She glances up at the clock. "Yes. I was just about to text you. I had a loose end to tie up first, and I was unsure how long it would take me, but I'm finished. We can go."

She unplugs her laptop and stuffs it in her satchel.

I reach for it. "I got this, Babe."

She smiles at me, and I swear my heart tries to float away. I lift my arm as she walks around her desk, and she slides underneath as natural as if she had done it a thousand times before. Her hand skims along the arch of my back and comes to rest on my waist as I hug her tight to me. "So ... Gold Coast Winery's tasting room?"

She tilts her face as we walk to Lucifer and the door. The warmth in her eyes stirs the lust in my loins, and I marvel at how she's always had that effect on me. "No. We would need a reservation for a private tasting room."

"Ah, you're breaking my heart."

"We're going to pick up an order to go from Lola's Diner and take it back to your place to eat."

Hell yeah! I would love to kiss the fuck out of her right now, but puckering my lips is impossible. My smile splits my face from ear to ear.

"I hope you have more than 30 minutes then."

She tries to bite her bottom lip, but her grin's too big too. "Sandy's given me permission to work remotely on the article for the contest."

I look back at Sandy, and she mouths, "You're welcome."

It pays to be a Monroe.

At the door, Jorja speaks to Lucifer, "Good morning, Luce."

He wags his tail but waits.

When I pull the door open, I suck my lips, "Psst," and he heels.

Before Jorja goes through, she gives him a good hard head rub, flopping his ears back and forth, and I swear he smiles.

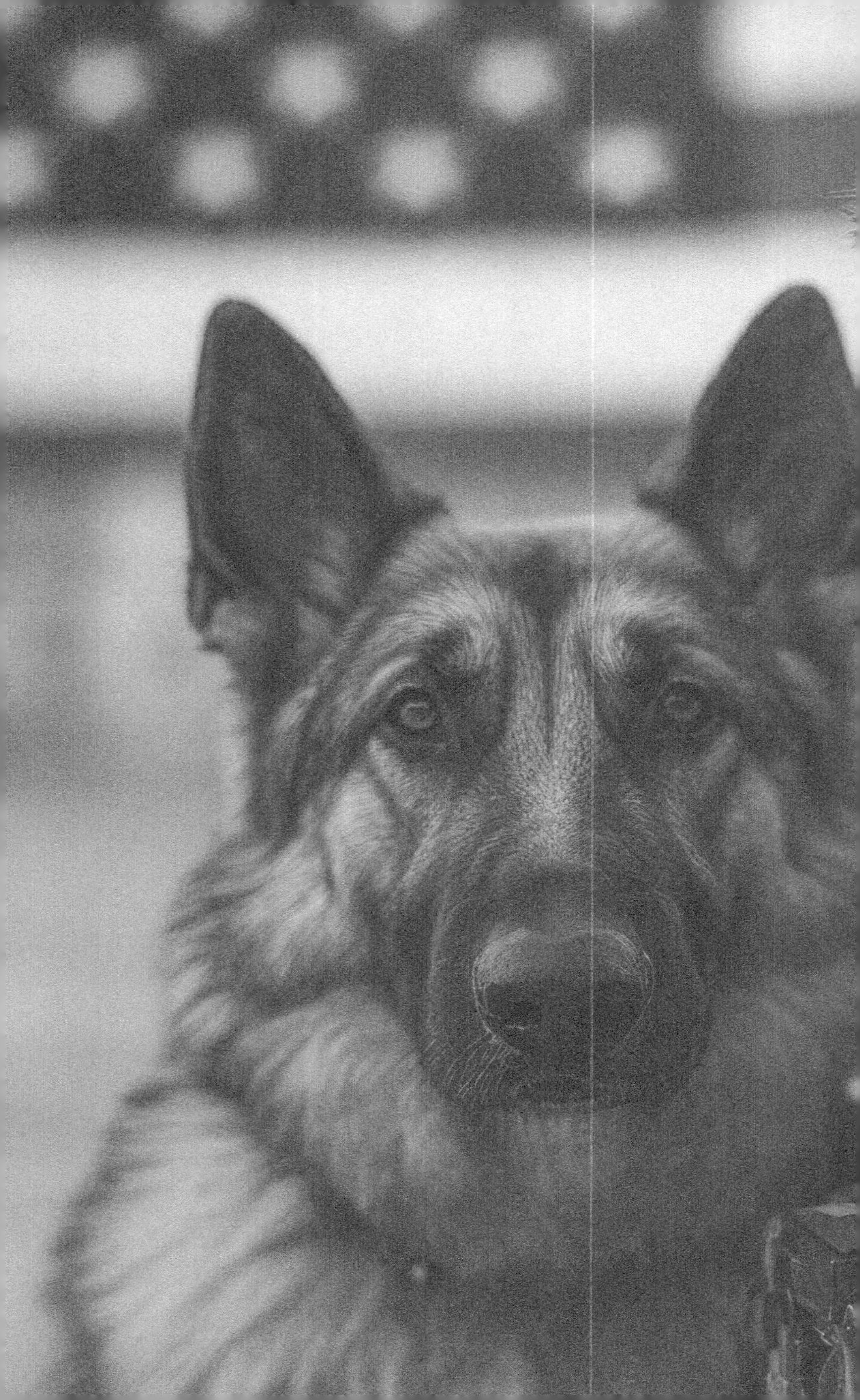

14

Jorja

I squint in the sunlight and shield my eyes with my hand as we step out of the building onto the sidewalk. Jocko takes my hand and steps off the curb, jaywalking across the street. His strides are long, so I tippy-toe run in my heels to keep up.

"Where did you park?"

He points, "Across the block."

"I can give you a lift over if you like."

"Not necessary."

But on the other side of the street, he turns toward my car.

"Jocko, are you going to walk me to my car?"

"Yes."

"Why?" I laugh. "For my safety?" I poke fun at him.

"No, for my sanity."

When we arrive, he spins me around and pushes me up

against it. My heart drops to my feet and lights that spark only he seems to be able to ignite.

He sets my satchel on the hood, then takes the flowers from my hand and throws them on top. Then his lips descend to mine as his hands feel their way around my hips to my ass.

I suck a deep breath of his essence as my body instantly submits to his desire. His lips crush mine as his hands grab a handful of my butt cheeks, and he lifts me off my heels. He wedges a knee between my legs, forcing them open. My tight skirt slides up my stockinged thighs as they spread for him. He sets me on the hood of the car and kisses the fuckity fuck out of my mouth, leaving no doubt to anyone, especially me, what his intentions are.

I slide my arms around his neck and make sure that everyone, from Jocko to my coworkers staring out the window, knows what my intentions also are.

When he finally lets me go, he stares into my dazed eyes. I am a hot mess, and he is too.

"My God, Jocko."

"I warned you I would be brazen the next time I kissed you."

I bite my bottom lip. "Yes, you did, but...."

"But ... you don't want me kissing you?"

"I did not say that."

"Then what are you saying?" His lips peck mine and the world spins again.

My voice is husky and breathy. "I am ready to feed you."

He picks my ass up and slides my hot mess down his hard body, then sets me on my feet. Stabilizes my weak knees. Grabs the flowers and my satchel, then pecks my lips again. Takes my hand. Sucks his lips, "Psst." And leads the way.

I blindly follow, not knowing where he is taking me and not caring because I will follow him to the ends of the earth.

When we round the corner at The Cottages, Live Oak's bed and breakfast, butterflies hit me. I know I'm ready, but I'm still nervous. He doesn't look at me as he unlocks the door. Holding my hand, he allows Lucifer to enter first, then we walk into the suite.

He tells Lucifer, "Crate up." And the K9 trots into the small bedroom. Jocko sets my satchel and the flowers down on a small table then takes me into his arms.

Without saying a word, his expression says everything. The longing and desire a clear and present danger to my virginity. "Jocko, I've never...." I let my words fade away.

His expression changes when my meaning registers. His look grows so intense, it takes my breath away. He cups my face between his hands, strokes it with his thumbs, and stares into my eyes. The love I see looking back at me stuns me. There's no longer any doubt in my mind how Jocko feels about me.

"Jorja, I can wait if you aren't ready."

"I didn't say that."

He leans down and kisses my forehead, then pulls me into his arms and holds me.

At first, I'm tense, nervous, but he doesn't do anything but hold me in his strong arms. Laying my cheek on his chest. Hearing his heart beating. Listening to his breath, moving in and out of his lungs. Feeling my face caress it as it does. The scent of his cologne teasing my nostrils. I feel safe, and slowly, I relax.

When I slide my hands around his waist and squeeze him, he kisses the top of my head. "Ham sandwich for lunch, or shall we order pizza?"

"Pizza," I whisper.

He shifts his embrace to one arm as he pulls his phone from his pants pocket and dials. "I would like an extra-large pineapple, mushroom, with black olives and pepperoni on a hand-tossed crust, please."

I lean back and look up at him. "You remember how I like my pizza?"

He winks. "Jocko Monroe. The Cottages. Suite One." Then he hangs up. "I remember everything about you."

"I know nothing about you."

"Shall we start the interview then?" Both arms hug me back against his body, and for the next fifteen minutes, he holds me while I ask him questions that any good interviewer would ask. Then I inquire why he joined the Navy instead of becoming a pro baseball player. His answer is short and to the point. "To make a difference in the world."

"Tell me about being a SEAL. Start with the training."

He begins with the 24 weeks of BUD/S, Basic Underwater Demolition/SEAL, training. Then explains there are another 26 weeks of SEAL Qualification Training. He gives some details, so I genuinely understand what "Hell Week" was like. The physical demands make my head spin, and I admire his body. He's a perfect specimen of masculinity. I listen, enthralled by it all, seeing him as the warrior.

While he reminisces, I notice that his right eyebrow has an involuntary twitch that is sexy as hell!

Somewhere during the interview, the pizza arrives. He gets a six-pack of beer from the mini-fridge, and we move to the couch.

He tells me about becoming a K9 handler, how he met

Lucifer, and the six months of extensive training they went through. He gives me a couple of examples, such as why barking isn't allowed.

"So, how do you train the dogs to jump from airplanes?"

"First, they either have it, or they don't."

I grin, "Lucifer has 'it' in droves. Just like you."

He grins, "We do love it."

"That isn't what I meant."

He winks, "I know what you meant."

Jocko brags how Lucifer was such a badass that other 'operators' requested him for missions. He tells me a couple of funny stories, then describes how proud he felt when Lucifer was awarded the Military Working Dog Service Award for Combat.

"And now I'm my shep's civilian dad." He finishes off his beer.

I stare at him in total amazement. "Wow, I had no idea!"

He laughs as he reaches for the empty pizza box and closes the lid. "Most people don't."

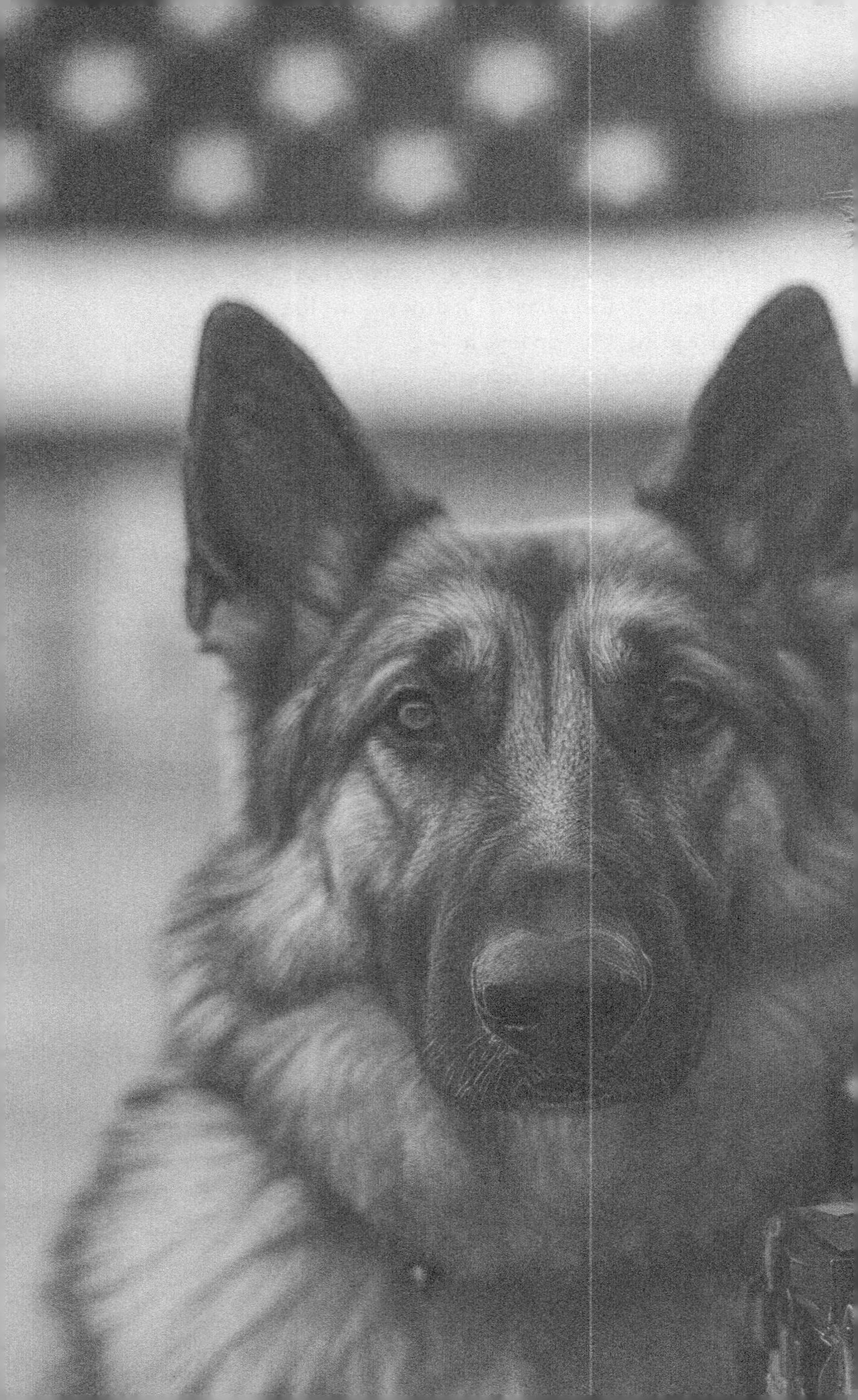

15

Jorja

I crawl over to him on the couch and push him back against the cushions, then straddle his lap. My skirt slides up, hugging my ass, exposing my black thigh-high stockings. He leans his head back and smirks. "I take it the interview is over?"

I nod as I begin unbuttoning my blouse.

His eyes crinkle at the corners, and his right eyebrow twitches. "You have moved from shock to awe?"

"I have." I grind him once to satisfy the hunger between my legs.

"Kiss me, Jorja." His hands push mine away and take over the task of unbuttoning my shirt.

I lean forward to kiss him as he pushes the fabric off. He opens his mouth, asking for my tongue, and I thrust it inside. He clamps down on it and sucks as his fingers quickly unclasp my bra. It falls away as his hands cup my breasts, massaging gently. He pinches the taut, elongated tips lightly, then pulls, flicking them. An exquisite surge of pleasure bursts inside me, and I moan against his mouth and grind against his erection.

His fingers travel down to my panties and run over the cold, wet spot covering my clit. Proof of how juicy he makes me. His fingers slip under the delicate fabric, and the sheer warmth of his skin sends another surge of pleasure through me. I arch my back and buck, wanting more. His mouth searches, sucking my skin where it lands until it finds a nipple and latches on.

Another jolt of pleasure.

Another reflexive buck.

He shifts the thin fabric exposing my entrance. All the while stroking my tender flesh around and around in a hypnotic rhythm of lust. Faster and faster, he pets my pussy holding my body captive with his suckling mouth on my tit. Until the only thing there is, is the aching need deep inside between my legs.

My unconscious pants and moans fill the room. My hands fondle his head. My fingers flex in his hair. Burning the vision of him doing that forever in my mind.

My cries of "Jocko, Jocko, please Jocko," falling on deaf ears as his titillating turns pure torturous. I beg him, bucking, shoving his shoulders back. The suction "pops" when the seal is broken. My tits dangle while I claw at his jeans clumsily. "I need you inside me."

He leans back into the couch and lifts his hips while his hooded eyes bore into mine, wearing an expression full of lust. My clit slides against his hard cock as he pushes my body down his legs while he unbuttons then unzips his jeans. My eyes are glued on his groin, remembering the size and thickness of his cock when I held it in the helicopter.

When it springs out, a moan escapes. "Oh my God, that thing is magnificent!" I grasp the head, run my hand down the length, enjoying the feel of the silky smoothness covering the rigid hardness, and my mouth waters. I go down on him as deep as I can without gagging, and his sharp intake of breath is satisfying. Sucking and licking his cock, I glance at his face. He's straining from the pleasure.

Our eyes connect, and he grabs my hair, pulling me off his cock, and back up to kiss his mouth. I thrust my tongue inside again as he rips my panties off like they are nothing.

I'm so turned on, I'm shaking. His hands cup my ass, and he pulls my cheeks apart, lifting my hips as he lowers his, lining up, then he drives his dick through my virginity.

There's a short burst of pain like ripping a band-aid off.

"OH!" I gasp, arching my back, but then the pleasure of his cock filling my void completely, and I sigh, finally satisfied.

He stops, watching me.

Sitting on his erection, looking down on his gorgeousness, I want to remember this moment forever. His eyes search mine, then he pulls my lips to his, kissing me the same way he kissed me the first time in the lockers, like a drowning man.

Slowly I begin to ride him, driven by a need and hunger so primal the pain is ignored. The pleasure dominating the discomfort.

With his hand working my hips and the other tickling my clit, my pussy becomes demanding. Faster and faster, I grind until my passion overwhelms reality. Moaning over and over again, pushing off his chest, working his cock in and out, I fuck him with abandon until I crash, whimpering with the explosion of wave after wave of orgasmic ecstasy.

Then I collapse onto Jocko's chest like a limp rag doll.

Jocko

Fucking A, Jorja. Fuck ... ing ... A, baby. You were worth coming back for.

Her curled, content body laying on mine is about as good as life gets. The way she fucked. Without reservation, letting go of all thoughts, moved by the moment, absolutely owning it. Yeah, she is a total badass.

I kiss her hair, then clear the stray strands covering her face. She's so beautiful. And Jesus Christ, she was still pure. I'm such a lucky ass.

She lifts her head to kiss my chest, then rolls onto her stomach. My fingers dance lightly down her back to the zipper on her skirt, and I push it down. As she drags her body over mine to stare into my eyes, I slip it over her ass.

Her arms trap my face as her fingers play in my hair. She studies my features. The tenderness I see looking at me proves how precious she is. She places butterfly kisses randomly on my face. Communicating without words.

The softness of her body, the sweetness of her essence, and the affection in her kisses reach the depths of my soul and fills my cock with a need to possess her.

Standing up, I cradle her tight, and her arms lock behind my head. Her skirt falls to the ground, then her legs wrap themselves around my waist while her eyes bore into mine.

We are both hungry for more.

I kick the bedroom door shut, then pull the bed sheet back and gently lay her down. "I want you naked."

She lays back on the bed and watches while I remove her heels and stockings. As I slowly undress, savoring the moment, she reaches for me.

Crawling to the middle of the bed, I kneel before her. She looks incredibly beautiful and vulnerable, with her hair fanning out on the white sheets and her big amber eyes full of lust, desire, and trust.

"You have the most beautiful sculpted lips, Jocko." She reaches to touch them, and I lean down so she can. Her fingers gently trace the edges, then she pushes one inside, and my tongue rolls over it, then wraps around it, and I suck. Her eyelids hood, and the sight makes everything inside harden with desire. I release the suction of it to flick it fast.

She smiles. "Is that how you're going to eat my cherry pie?"

I grin as I go down on her, and her finger slips out.

"That's affirmative."

She smiles as she puts her finger in her mouth, and lets me see her tongue wrap around it, then she sucks it.

God, this woman! My balls tighten, and my cock goes rigid. Grabbing her ankles, I pull her body into position, then push her legs apart. Her slit is small and pink. I push my hands under her hips and lift her pussy to my lips. Her legs splay open.

Nipping, licking, sucking her inner thigh, I work my way up to taste her tenderness. When I reach her perfect pink little slit, I drag my long, flat tongue from bottom to top, leaving nothing neglected.

Her breath hitches, then she moans. The sound makes my cock throb.

I take my time eating her entire treasure. Her hips hunch, helping, while her fingers flex in my hair, pulling me down, then pushing me off, riding my tongue. Her moans become a song.

Her face fills with passion, then contorts with pleasure as I bring her to the brink. Flicking my tongue fast over her clit, her legs begin to quiver.

Gripping her hips tight, I hold her still. Sucking her. Flicking her. Driving her. Wanting to hear her scream with pleasure. She arches her back, thrusting her tits to the ceiling.

She's close. So close. Come on, baby, come on. Give it to me.

Then she grips the bedsheets. "UUUgh! Jocko! Baby! Slam that monster in me! Give it to me, DEEP! PLEASE!"

Goddamn! My cock floods with blood. My balls fill to the brink. Pre-cum oozes out. And all self-control is gone!

I push off her, line it up, and give her what she wants.

I slam my monster to the fucking hilt into her tight, velvet, juicy pussy, pulling a groan of sheer rapture from my mouth. She grabs my bulging triceps to hold on as she cries her encouragement, "YES, YES!"

The mattress bounces with the force of the fucking, and her mouth forms a silent "O" as I thrust with a frenzy. Her face scrunches tighter and tighter as my cock gets harder and harder. When I cum, the power of my ejaculation deep into her rolls her eyes back, and her whole body convulses with her orgasm.

I collapse on top of her, unable to move, and we breathe face to face. Helpless, happy, minds fucking blown.

She recovers first and begins pecking my lips with sweet, little butterfly kisses.

I force my eyes open and drape my arm around her. Her happiness beams at me, making me smile. Totally content for the first time in my life, I close my eyes and sleep.

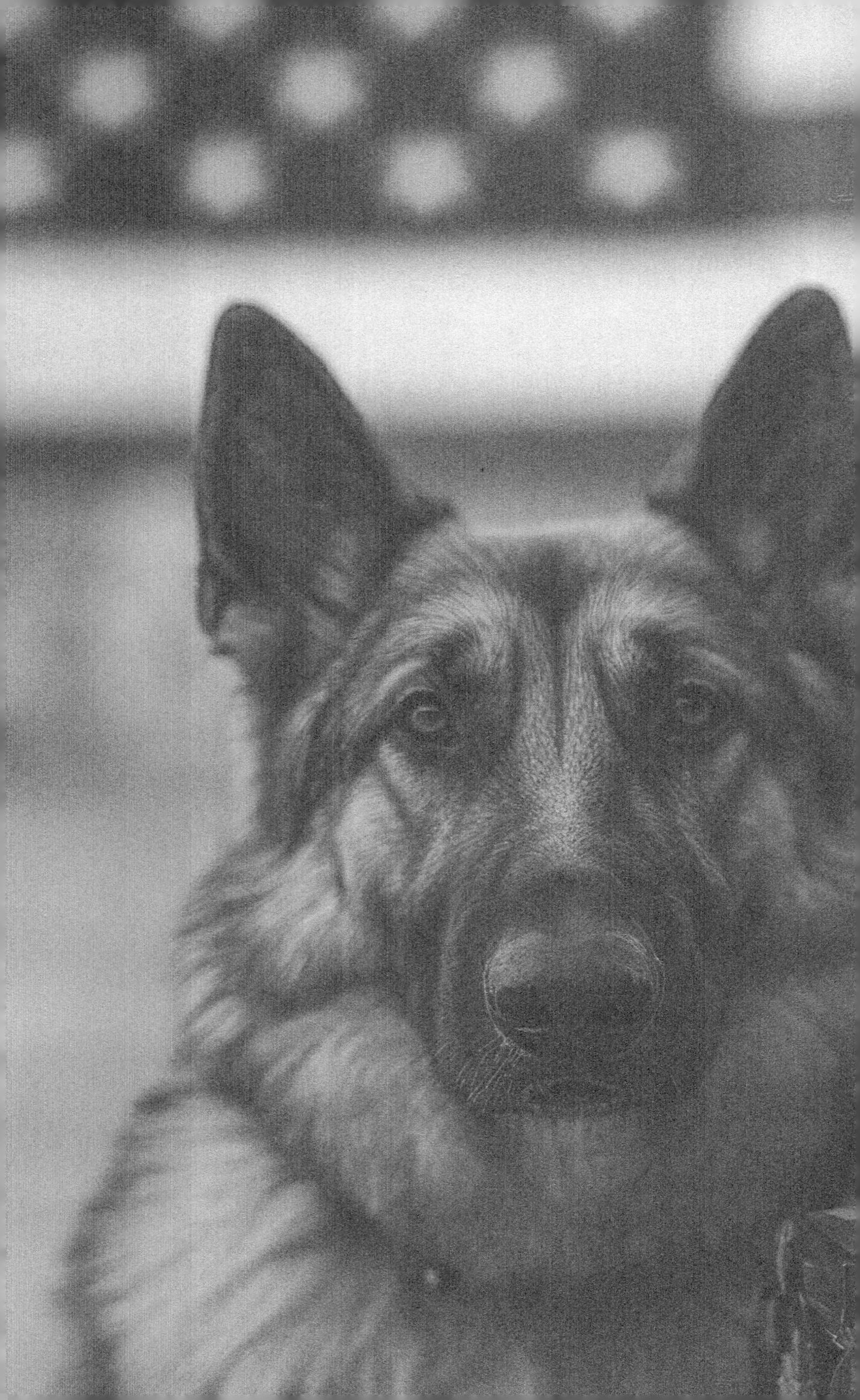

16

Jocko

When I wake, I reach for Jorja, but she isn't in bed. Sitting up, I glance around for her clothes. Her heels and hose lay abandoned on the floor, and I drop back on the bed and stretch. I hear the toilet flush and reach for a pillow to prop my head up so I can fully enjoy the vision I'm about to see.

She opens the door slowly and peeks out. I can't help the grin plastered on my face.

With her hair bound up in a towel, she walks to the bed. Her naked body's rosy red from a hot shower, but it's her eyes and her smile that captivates me. She looks different.

I lift my hand, "Come here."

Crawling to me, her tits dangling, I'm naturally tempted to cup them, but her eyes keep me focused. I touch her shoulder and trace my fingers down her arm. She gives me her hand, and I hold it. "Are you okay?"

She nods. "I've never been better."

Leaning forward, she kisses me. I cup her face and let her tenderness reach those dark places I've hidden from the world.

When she lets my lips go, she stares into my eyes, tracing her fingertips along my lips, pulling my bottom lip out, and popping it. She smiles, "If I'm dreaming, please don't wake me."

I bring her hand to my lips, kissing the back, then flip it over to kiss the palm. She spreads her fingers and cinches our hands, then kisses them. She shakes the towel off and rolls into my embrace.

"Ditto." I kiss the top of her head.

We lay content in silence. My thoughts go back to the first time I saw her and fell in love.

I was a sophomore, and she was a freshman. It was the first day of school, and I was sitting in the gym with my bros, cutting up, cackling at the freshman girls, giving the newbies nicknames that would stick the remainder of their lives. Some were brutal, some were funny, but none were nice.

Then Jorja walked in. Her long hair was curled and bounced. Her bangs pulled into a ponytail. Her body was built like a brick shit house.

She was wearing a red ribbed sweater tank top with a choker collar that accentuated her curves. Her tits were full, but not excessive. She had on a pair of skinny jeans with heels. Her legs were long, her thighs curvy, and her ass was perfectly proportional. The guys gave her all sorts of appropriate names, like Ten for the Win and Dick Flick, but I was quiet. Actually, I was speechless. Surprised that just looking at her made me feel good inside.

She passed by totally ignoring us, but I continued to stare at her climbing the bleachers, daintily threading the crowd, being polite. It wasn't until she sat down that she looked at our group, and our eyes connected. At that moment, time stood still, and I knew she was going to be mine.

One of the guys, I don't remember who now, ribbed me and asked. "So, what are we going to call her?"

I grinned at him. "I'm calling, 'Dibs.'"

"Fuck!" He whined, "That's not what I meant."

"But that's what it is."

The others complained, but I just stared at her, amazed that a girl could evoke such an emotional reaction.

Two hours later, I was pulled from class and told my parents had been killed in an auto accident, and everything changed.

She looks at me. "When did you know?"

I grin, "I was just remembering when."

She flips over, expectantly. Her eyes are shining.

"When did *you* know?" I tease her, knowing she wants me to go first but making her confess before I do.

"I think I knew the first time I saw you." She lays her head on my chest, and absentmindedly runs her fingertips over my skin. Circling my trident scar, she asks, "What happened here?"

"That's from my Budweiser."

"A Budweiser gave you a scar?"

"Not the beer. That's what we call our trident."

"Trident?"

"It's the medal that says you're a SEAL."

"And you have a scar from it?"

"The ceremony isn't a pinning; it's a pounding."

"Oh, my word!"

"It's a badge of honor, Babe. I'm proud as hell to be

branded." I bring the subject back to our discussion of when. "So, the first day of school then?"

She kisses my scar before she speaks, and the gesture fills me with pride.

"Yes. I stood in the doorway of the gym and scanned the crowd looking for a place to sit. I didn't know anyone, and I didn't want to walk all the way to the other side because there was this group of guys heckling some of the girls. But then I saw you sitting there. You were laughing. You were the cutest guy I had ever seen." She glances up at me. "Before I realized what I was doing, I was walking out. The closer I got to your group, the more nervous I was. I prayed the whole way that I wouldn't get a horrid name, but if I did and you noticed me, I knew it would be worth it."

"Oh, I noticed you! When you walked by in that tight red sweater tank top with your beautiful tits and those tight jeans that proved your ass was perfect too, I was done. I couldn't take my eyes off you."

She pushes up, and I pull her to my lips.

"But then a day or so later, I overheard you brutally cussing out a girl, and I didn't want any part of a dude that was that mean."

"I was never mean to you."

"I didn't see the difference. You were hateful to her, therefore...."

"I'm not proud of treating any of them that way, you know. But I did what I had to do."

"It was over the top."

"Was it? Do you know why I had to resort to being that damn crude?"

She frowns, and her eyes narrow. "No ...."

"They were grab-assing my junk."

"What?"

"It's true. When the size of my cock became the envy of the locker room, word got out, and there were a few girls who copped a feel to confirm it."

Her mouth falls open.

"I'm not shitting you. Those were the girls I cussed out."

"Oh, my god!" She dies laughing. "Of all the things you could have said, that wasn't what I was expecting!"

"I took care of it the best way I knew how."

"Why didn't you tell someone?"

"That isn't exactly something I wanted to broadcast to the whole school." I sweep my hand across the air, "Jocko Monroe, sexually harassed by groping girls."

She giggles.

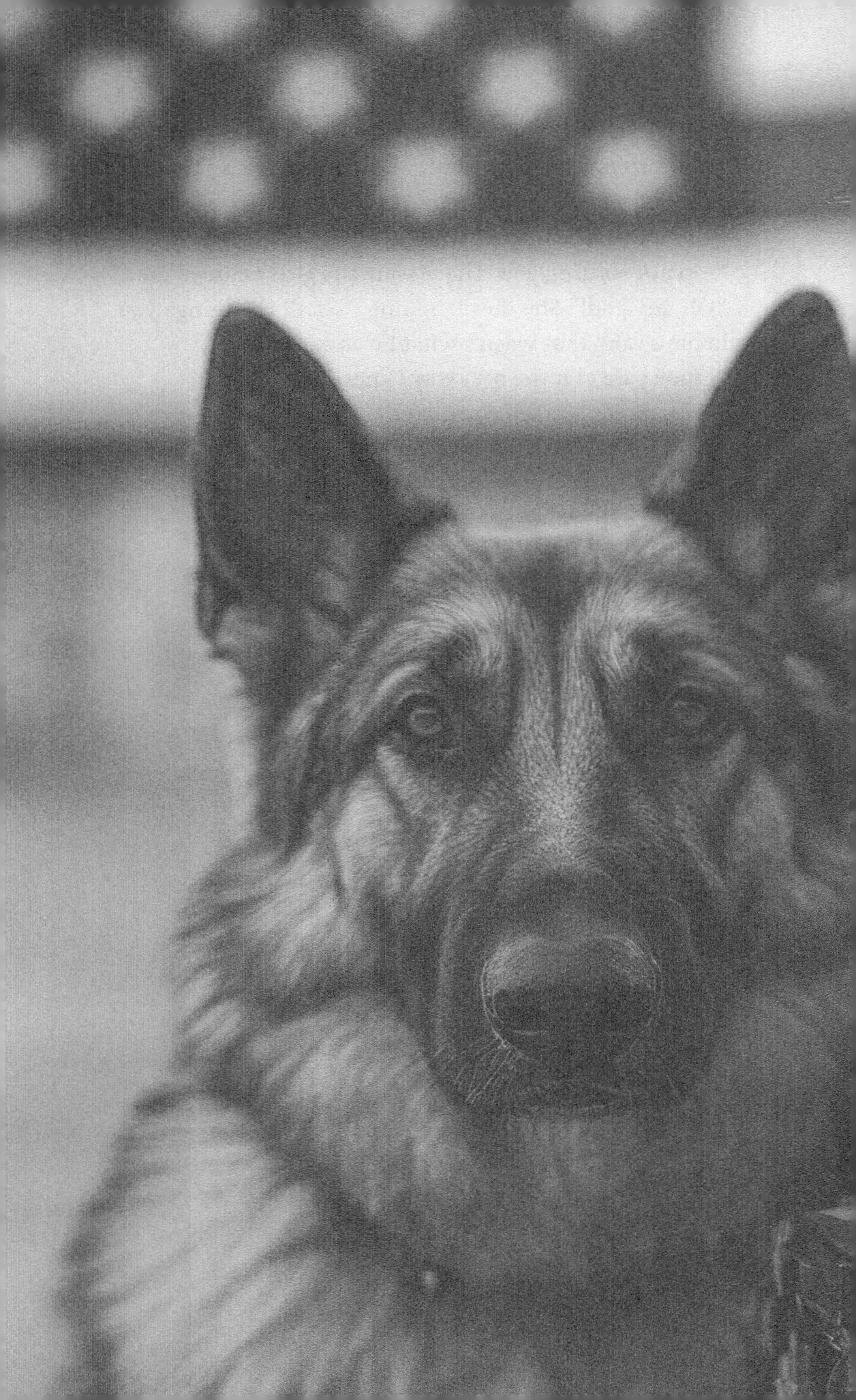

17

Jocko

After a nice hot shower, I open the bathroom door. Jorja isn't in bed, so I wrap the towel around my waist and look for her in the living room. She's dressed and sitting on the couch with Lucifer. His head is in her lap, and she's petting him, talking to him. The look on his face mirrors mine. He's completely content.

When I enter the room, they both look up at me. "I hope you don't mind. He looked so lonely in his cage."

"He's got the big puppy dog eyes down pat, doesn't he?"

She smiles and ruffs his neck. "Yes, he does. But he's such a good boy!"

Shaking my head, I walk back in to get dressed. She comes to the door to watch. "I was thinking we should go grab a bite to eat. What's your favorite food? Italian? Mexican?"

"American. I'm a steak and potatoes man."

"Of course you are." She smirks. "There's Angelo's steakhouse we could hit."

"Sounds good."

"I'll call ahead and make sure Lucifer's allowed." She takes her phone and walks back to him on the couch.

Walking back into the room, pulling my shirt over my head, my phone dings. She glances at it but doesn't say anything. But her expression changes, and she bites her bottom lip. Picking it up, I see why.

> Do we have a date tonight or not? I need to know what to wear. Sexy and available?

I walk over to Jorja. "Hey, whatever you just thought, let it go." I wrap my arms around her. "Don't assume the worst, okay? Let me explain. We have to be able to communicate, or this won't work."

She rests her face on my chest.

"Demi's a big flirt, but she's also an old friend."

"Like Liz?"

"No, Liz is just a big flirt." I laugh. "Demi's a friend. I stopped by her place earlier this week because I need her help with Lucifer. He needs to socialize with other dogs. She wanted to hear some war stories and invited me —us, for a beer tonight at nine at The Stallion. If you don't want to go, we won't."

"That didn't sound like I was invited."

"Here, I'll prove it."

I text Demi.

> BFF's. See you there.

> JORJA'S A LUCKY GIRL. DON'T BE LATE.

Walking across the parking lot with Jorja's satchel on my shoulder and the flowers in her hand, she tells me a little about what she did after high school. She shares that her mother married the next year and moved to Arizona. She rented the house from her and started working at the magazine instead of going off to college. She earned her degree working during the day and taking online classes. When we reach her car, I give her another long kiss, then open the door.

She slides in, looks up at me, shields her eyes with her hand, and says, "Are you sure Lucifer will be alright in the hotel room alone?"

I smirk. "I'm sure. He'll climb up on the bed and sleep."

"Okay, I'll pick you up at eight then."

I watch her pull away, standing there until she's out of sight.

I look down at my boy. "Do you realize she's going to be your mama?"

He wags his tail, and we head for my truck. The businesses are all closed, so the hike's short. When we're loaded, I ask him. "We've got an hour to kill. Want to go to the park and chase the ball?"

Jorja

Standing in my closet trying to decide what to wear tonight is pure torture. The Stallion is not a fancy place. It's a redneck bar. I should wear casual clothes and Converse tennis shoes. But Demi's text makes me stop. She was going to wear sexy and available.

I grab my phone.

> Macey! Help!

>> WHAT'S WRONG? ARE YOU OKAY?

> I NEED TO KNOW WHICH DRESS SAYS SEXY AND AVAILABLE.

>> AH! AN EASY CHOICE. THE LITTLE BLACK DRESS. YOU KNOW, THE ONE YOU HAVEN'T WORN?

>> WHERE IS JOCKO TAKING YOU?

I slide the hangers until I'm looking at it stuffed in the very back of my clothes. It was a drunk purchase. It's mostly spandex and leaves nothing to the imagination. Hanging there, it looks like a tube top.

> We are going out to eat at Angelo's, then to The Stallion. Are you sure about that dress?

>> GIRL, YOUR BODY OWNED THAT DRESS. IT OOZES SEX AND SCREAMS AVAILABLE.

> I DON'T KNOW. I WANT SEXY, NOT WHORE.

>> WHEN YOU ARE GOING AFTER A MAN, GO WHORE! TRUST ME! EVERY MAN WANTS TO TAKE A GIRL HOME THAT PROMISES WHAT THAT DRESS PROMISES. JOCKO WON'T TAKE HIS EYES OFF YOU. NOT JUST BECAUSE HE'S HORNY FOR YOU BUT BECAUSE EVERY OTHER MAN IN THERE WILL BE DROOLING OVER YOU. AND HE WON'T LIKE THAT.

I laugh, remembering poor Joseph Pruitt in high school.

> Very strategic.

Exactly!

Thank you!

That's what besties do.

I take the dress off the rack.

> Leave your hair casual. Down and uncurled.

Not up?

No. When your hair's up, you look very sophisticated. Definitely down.

Sophisticated? Hmm, I'll wear it up for Angelo's, then down at The Stallion.

> Okay.

I just bought a pair of gold platforms. Want to borrow them?

Ha! That's pushing the sexy look a little too far toward whore.

> No, thank you. I'll wear stilettos.

The red ones?

> No. The black ones with the ankle strap and zipper.

Those work. Red lipstick. Red strapless bra. No stockings. No panties

> No panties?

> **BARE NAKED BOOTY BABY!**
>
> ONCE JOCKO KNOWS THAT LITTLE SECRET, HE'LL BE HARD ALL NIGHT, AND THE SEX LATER WILL BE SMOKIN'!
>
> SO, THIS AFTERNOON? DID HE TAKE YOUR CROWN?

> HE HAD ALL MY CHERRY PIE.

> AH! FINALLY! I'LL CALL YOU TOMORROW. YOU CAN TELL ME EVERYTHING.

> LOVE YOU, BOO. THANK YOU.

> YEP. LOVE YOU TOO. HAVE FUN!
>
> HEY! ONE LAST THING. DON'T GET WASTED! I WANT TO KNOW EVERYTHING THAT HAPPENS.

> HAHA. NO GUARANTEES.

I go into the bathroom and turn the water on in the tub. I need to soak my pounded pussy in a nice hot bath. Jocko is big, and I know I'm going to be sore.

After pouring in some coconut-scented Epsom salt, I ease in. "Ah, that'll make it all better down there."

An hour later, I am dressed in the sexiest dress I have ever worn, with my hair piled on top of my head, looking at myself in the mirror and realizing I'll turn heads tonight. But knowing, the only one that matters is Jocko's.

I take one last look around and straighten the flowers he gave me in the vase. I set them by the front door, so they will be the first thing I see when I walk in and the last thing I see when I leave.

A sweet reminder of Jocko's commitment and a warning not to fuck it up again.

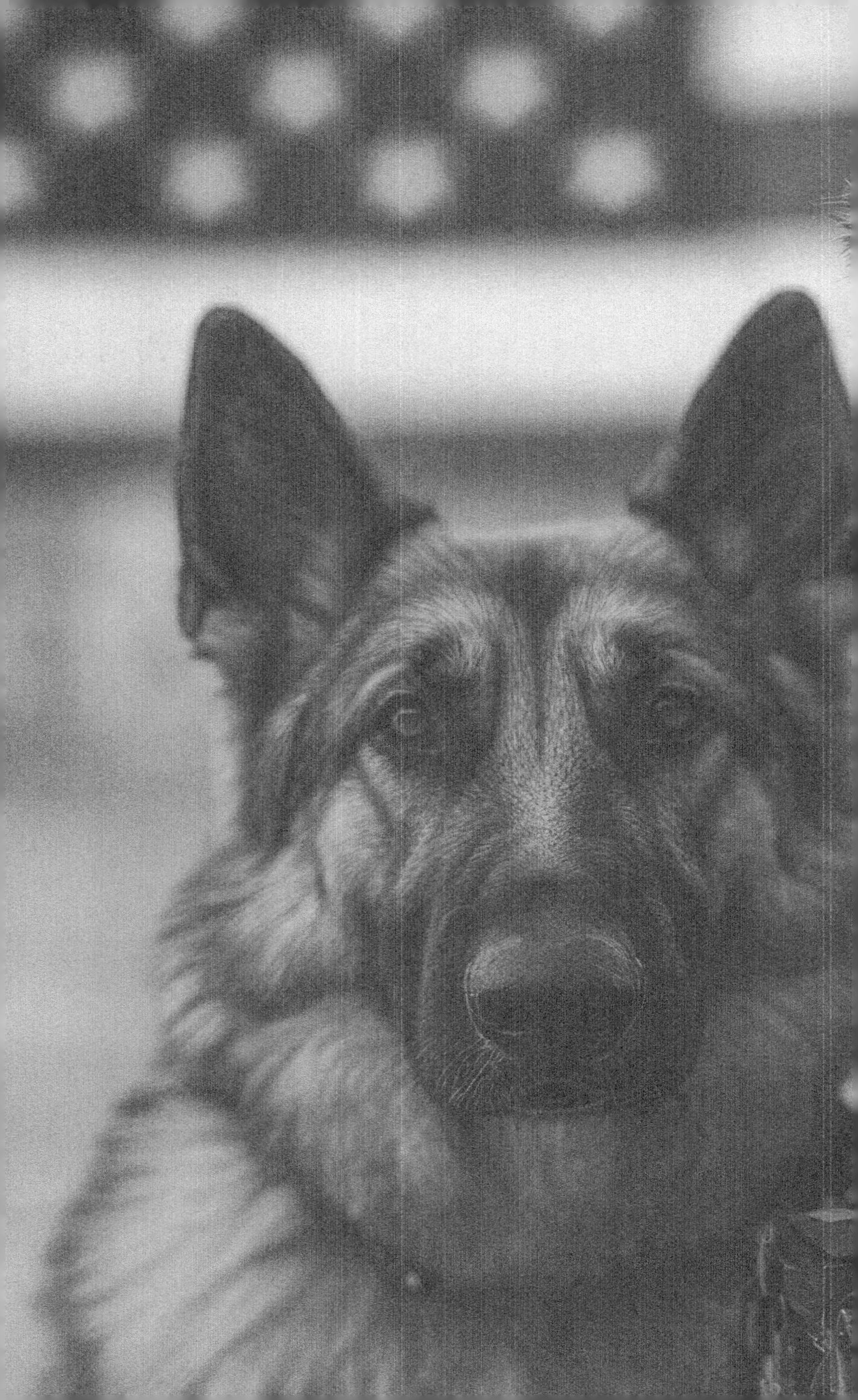

18

Jocko

She's wearing a very short little black dress that shows off her long legs and every perfect curve of her body, and I turn in the seat to stare at her. "You look stunning, Juicy."

"Thanks." She grins as she puts her car in drive and pulls out onto the highway. "Are you sure Lucifer will be alright until we come ...." She stops, catching herself before she says, home?

Grinning like I've won the grand prize at the fair, I assure her. "He's a dog. He'll be fine. He'll sleep."

As she weaves through the traffic, I stare at her. Each time she cuts her eyes and sees I'm still looking at her, she smiles.

"Yes, I can't take my eyes off you."

"Good." She says as she turns into Angelo's Steakhouse. As soon as she's parked, I ask her. "May I open the door for you?"

"Certainly."

I jump out, trot around, and make a big deal about opening her door, offering my hand, and pulling her to her feet. "I would kiss you right now, but...."

"But we need to eat before we go out drinking."

"Yes, that too."

She hooks my arm, and I escort her inside.

When I pull open the door, Jorja glides through, and the hostess looks up. Her eyes skip right over Jorja and light up when they meet mine. I've seen the look too many times before not to recognize a single woman looking to score.

When we walk up to her, she asks me for my name, but before I can give it, Jorja asserts herself and tells her, "Jorja Jones."

The hostess takes two menus and leads us to our table. I pull the chair out for Jorja, and she beams up at me as she sits. "I like this gentlemanly side to you."

"I fucking love the lady look, Babe."

She chuckles, "Spontaneous drunken shopping spree success."

The waitress appears. "Welcome to Angelo's. Do you need a drink menu?" She looks from me to Jorja.

"Water, please," Jorja says.

"Coors."

"Coming right up."

Looking over the menu, I prepare Jorja. "Just so you aren't shocked, I eat my steak very rare."

"No worries. I like mine rare too." She continues to read the pages.

"Mine will bleed."

She looks up and shrugs, "Okay." Then goes back to reading the menu. I'm still staring at her when she closes it. "What?"

"I'm just amazed."

"At the fact that I won't freak out at the sight of blood oozing from the steak when you stab it?"

I laugh. "Well ... yeah."

She laughs with me. "I'll have the Dallas filet, small cut, with a Caesar salad, no croutons."

I smirk. "This is my treat. You can have anything on the menu."

She smirks back. "It's not your treat. It's mine. I invited you, and I'm not concerned with the price. That's what I want to eat." She places her hands on the table and leans over it to tell me, "*You* can have anything on the menu *you* want, and that includes dessert."

"And just like that, I'm not in charge." I laugh, looking back at the choices.

She laughs.

When the waitress returns with our drinks, I give her our order, and she takes the menus.

Jorja smiles at me and says, "Just in case I forget later on, or we get too drunk to remember, I had a really good time tonight."

"You're too sweet, and I did too." I slide my hand across the table, and she sets hers in it. I stroke it with my thumb, enjoying the touch of her skin.

We chat about all sorts of frivolous things, just getting to know each other. I learn she doesn't really watch much TV, and I tell her I don't either. She reads a lot, which is good because I do too. She reads romance and likes action and adventure. We discuss our favorite authors, and when I ask her, "Would you like to go to a book signing this year?"

Her mouth falls open, and flips the switch that causes my cock to harden. This is going to be a long night.

"I would love to! It's on my bucket list!"

"It's a date then to anywhere you want to go."

The waitress brings our food, and it takes me twice as long as it does Jorja to eat. She laces her fingers, puts her elbows on the table, and watches me eat. True to her word, she doesn't flinch when I cut the steak and the blood oozes onto the plate.

"You're an animal, you know." She grins.

"Yeah. I know." I smirk, stab it, and consume it.

When we're finished, she slides her credit card to me, but I slide it back. We stare at each other, then she submits, and damn, my cock fills again.

Jorja

Jocko opens the door for me at The Stallion. The sounds of a large crowd having fun and letting go of the workweek's stress rush out. I hesitate, and he puts his hand in the curve of my back. I look up at him from under my lashes, tilt my head, release the clip in my hair, shake it out, pull the top of my dress down another inch or so, hike the hem up more than a couple of inches, and tease him. "By the way, I'm not wearing any panties."

The look on his face is priceless. Macey was right again. He won't be thinking about anything else for the rest of the night.

There's a banner stretched behind the bar that reads, "Welcome Home, Jocko!"

As he follows me in, he's hampered by people welcoming him home.

Demi waves from the bar, and when I reach her, she whistles. "Damn, girl! You clean up good!"

"Thanks." I grin at her. "I was hoping for that reaction."

"What will you have to drink? I'm picking up the tab tonight."

"I'll have a piña colada."

She flags the bartender down and gives him my order. He glances at me, and his eyes roam, then he grins. "Coming right up."

"Down, Dusty. She's with Jocko."

"Dammit." He says to her, then winks at me before he spins around to make my drink.

Demi asks as she nods toward Jocko. "How is he?"

"Good. Why do you ask?"

"He was always a hard nut to crack." We watch him thread his way to us. "I was wondering how much being a Navy SEAL had changed him. The job wasn't exactly a picnic."

Dusty delivers my drink, and she takes it from him, initials the tab, then hands it to me.

"Honestly, Demi, I wouldn't know. I barely knew him in school."

She cuts her eyes at me. "But I thought you two were...."

"Not back then."

"But now?"

I smile as he breaks free of the crowd and stands glaring at me ten feet away. His eyes are devouring me, knowing I'm bare down there.

"You tell me?"

She clinks my drink with hers. "Now is all that matters, girl. You grab that bull by the balls."

"Balls to the wall."

"You better believe it."

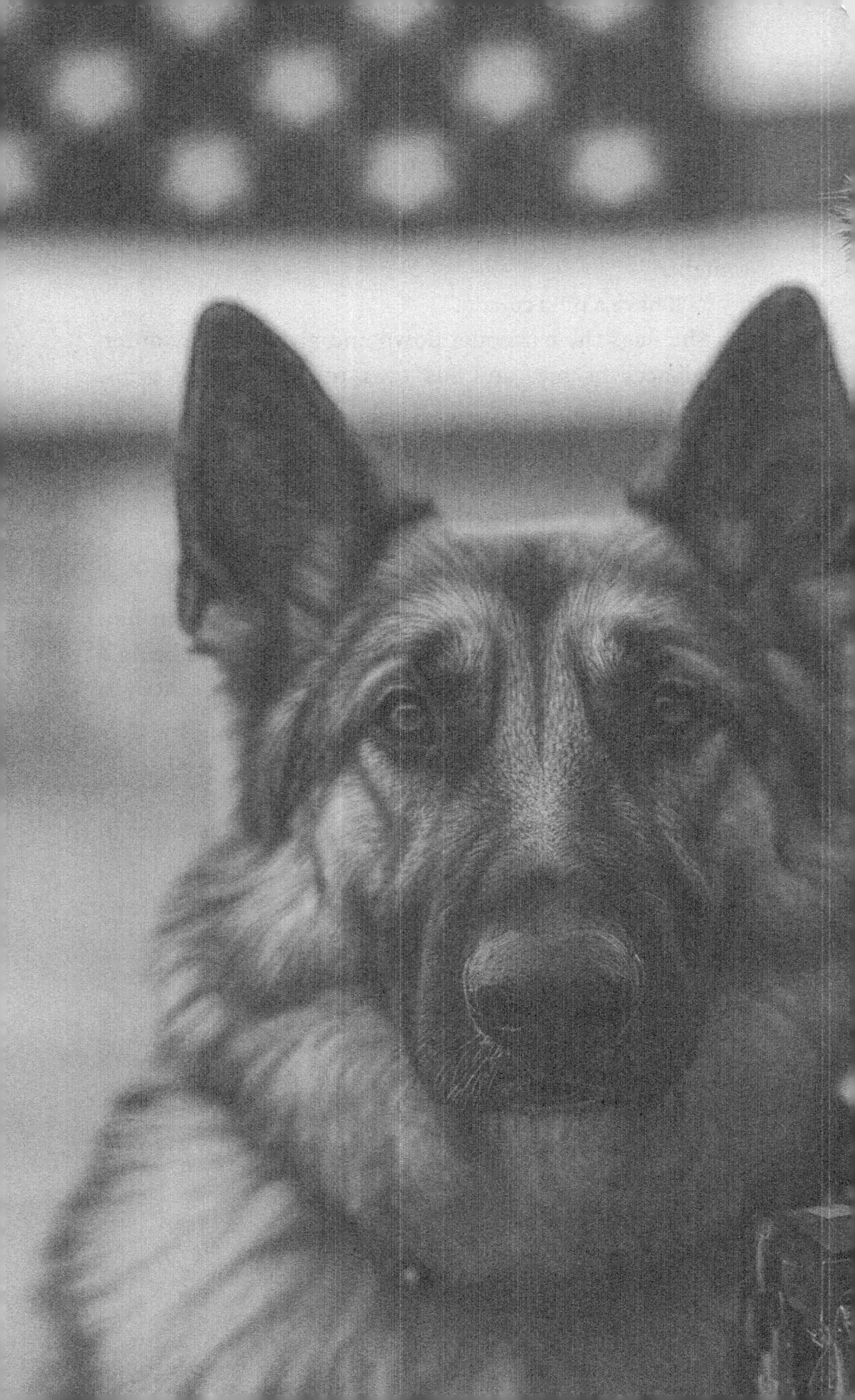

19

Jocko

The little minx sits on the barstool with her legs uncrossed, teasing me with the darkness between her thighs. They're talking about me from the looks on their faces, and when Demi clinks her glass, I wonder what they've plotted.

"Here's the hero." Demi teases as she puts her arm around me. "Drinks are on the house tonight."

The bartender leans over for my order. "What'll ya have?"

Demi puts her hand on his shoulder and climbs onto the bar.

"What are you doing?" I shake my head. "Get down from there."

She grins as Jorja tells the bartender. "Coors."

"Draft?"

Demi walks to the other end away from me as Jorja's hand slips into mine. The softness of her skin begs for my attention, and I turn to her. She's leaning forward on the stool, her tits jutting out, as she tilts her head all the way back to look up into my eyes.

God, I am going to fuck her brains out later.

She asks, "Draft or bottle?"

"Bottle. If a fight breaks out, I'll have a weapon."

The bartender's face goes slack for a split second before he regains his composure, then he gives me a thumbs-up and disappears.

Jorja laughs out loud.

"You think I'm joking?"

She smirks.

"Trust me, Babe. As hot as you look tonight, it's a real possibility."

Her eyes shine as a sweet smile spreads across those perfect lips, and I can't stand it any longer. I kiss her.

"Ladies and gentlemen, plus all you other bitches and bastards." Demi begins, and Jorja releases my hand and places it on my chest. I growl when she applies pressure, making her giggle, but I let her go.

Demi walks with her glass in the air. "Raise your drinks, and let's give a warm welcome home...." She points to me, "to Live Oak's *Very* Special Operator Jocko Monroe."

The bar raises their drinks as one, and Dusty slides my beer across the bar. I snatch it up, lift it high, and shout. "HOOYAH!"

Silence falls over the room as everyone drinks their salute, then the noise from the chatter kicks back off.

Demi squats down in front of me and laughs to my face. "That wasn't so bad now, was it?" She holds her arms out to me, and I lift her up, setting her on the ground.

Someone pats me on the back, and I turn to see who.

"Welcome back, brother. My name's Matthew. I served as an MPC handler with the Marines."

I nod. "Hooyah."

"Oorah. I run a dog training facility. You're welcome to bring your fur missile anytime and let him work."

"Thanks, man. I appreciate that. I'll take you up on it."

"No problem. It will help you both with the transition. I'm over on West Gate and Fourth." He slaps me on the back again and disappears into the mix.

Demi pats the empty stool between her and Jorja. "I'm ready for some war stories."

"I'm not sitting there. I'm sitting here." I hug Jorja from behind, wrapping my arm around her, then lifting her up, sliding onto her stool, and setting her on my lap.

She squeals, giggling.

"Be still. I don't want to drop you."

"Slick move there, hotrod." Someone says behind me. It's Coach Evers, my high school baseball coach. He reaches out, pats me on the back, gives me his Army, "Hooah," nods his head to Jorja, then turns his attention on Demi. "Is this seat available then? I'm all about war stories."

She nods. "Sure. Why not."

Coach served two tours, so we talk about teamwork, and the stories flow smoothly from baseball battles to combat. People stop to speak, and some buy me a drink. As an operator, I rarely overindulged, but tonight, I make an exception and accept more drinks than I should.

Jorja starts to squirm, then finally interrupts. "I hate to miss a single word, but I have to visit the ladies' room." She wiggles off my lap and disappears before Demi can offer to go with her.

My attention splits immediately. Watching her thread through the crowd, politely asking to pass if she gets stalled, turning the heads of the men as she goes. When she enters the bathroom and disappears from my sight, I turn back to a grinning Coach and Demi.

Coach informs me. "I just want you to know, if you hadn't come back to that girl, I would have kicked your ass."

I laugh, knowing he would've made good on that. I glance back at the bathroom. "My only regret when I left Live Oak was that I didn't take her with me."

Joseph Pruitt walks up. "I'm just glad I knew to back the fuck off."

"Sup, JP?" I hold out my hand, and he shakes it. "Welcome back, Jocko."

Jorja

Dear Lord. I pray, standing in line waiting for a stall to open. *Please do not let me pee my pants because I don't have any panties to pee on. It will literally run down my leg!*

Reaching out, I brace against the wall. I didn't realize I was so tipsy until I stood up. Trying to take my mind off my full bladder, I focus on what a group of girls are saying.

"Jocko Monroe is a fucking stud!"

"My God, he was gorgeous before he left, but now ... he is FUCKING gorgeous!"

"Makes me miss my Frog Hog days, girls."

"Frog hog? What the fuck is that?"

"SEAL whores." She laughs. "Why do you think I went to college in San Diego? It wasn't for the book education."

"Damn!"

"Yeah. It was the highlight of my college days."

"Are they good lovers?"

"Naw.... They're great fuckers, though!"

The girls laugh.

"Every weekend, a group of five of us would go down to a bar called, *Suds After BUD/S* and pick up one to take out back."

"Are they all as good-looking as Jocko?"

"Nooooo.... They aren't all hunks like him, but they all have that sexy as fuck, alpha male confident attitude that makes them stand out in a crowd."

"Babs! What's taking so long? Come on!"

Babs yells from a stall, "Don't leave me." The toilet flushes. She staggers out, and I hurry in. Barely getting my dress hiked as I squat, I forget about what they've said as the joy of peeing clears all thoughts from my brain.

But as soon as I walk out of the bathroom, I remember their conversation. The blood drains from my face, and I sober up instantly. Two of the girls are at the bar talking to Jocko. One's sitting on the stool Coach Severs was on, and the other is standing between her and Jocko. My gut feels sick as I stare. Their flirting is over the top, and Jocko smiles at them as he sips his beer.

Another woman comes out of the bathroom, so I slide to the side, looking for Demi. She's in Coach's arms dancing, and from the looks of how close, she doesn't intend to listen to more of Jocko's war stories tonight.

When I look back at the bar, the bartender delivers three shots, and my heart joins my stomach. They are definitely making a play for him. The girl seated pushes the third shot to Jocko and says something as she lifts her glass, encouraging him to toast with them.

My imagination fills in a 'threesome.'

He stares at it, not drinking it, but not refusing it either.

The little voice inside my head begins to scream. "Git yo ass in gear, gurl!"

Threading my way through the crowd, I try to decide how to behave when I confront them. Should I be the protective sassy bitch, or the silent smug snob?

I catch a glimpse of the girl standing with her hand resting on his shoulder, and my gut tightens. She must have said something because he turns to look at her. She tosses her hair and gives him a smile with an open invitation.

Just when I break through from the crowd, he picks the shot up, clinks theirs with his, and they all toss it back.

I freeze, feeling betrayed.

Jocko stands up, drains his beer, puts a tip on the bar, says something to them, turns, and comes face to face with me.

His sexy as fuck grin slides across his mouth. "Ah, there's my girl!" He raises his arm, reaching for me, wanting me to slide underneath. Absolutely no guilt on his face. "I was coming to look for you."

I hesitate for a split second, then decide on no drama. At least, not now. I walk into his embrace, and he tilts my face to his, tucks a strand of stray hair behind my ear, then kisses my forehead.

He turns me to the girls. "Hogs, meet the reason I'm out of the game. Juicy, these are Frog Hogs on the hunt."

None of us speak, they sneer at me, and I glare at them.

"Juicy's going to take my lucky ass home with her so I can fuck her brains out. Aren't you, B. A. E?"

Before Anyone Else. My heart melts. I put my arm around his waist, hug him tight, smashing my tits into his chest, and declare, "Yes, I am."

"You're mine. You know that, don't you?"

The possession in his eyes sends a wave of desire through me, and I answer truthfully. "I do. Do you?"

He crushes my body against his. "Let's get out of here."

As we weave our way through the crowd, "Baby I'm Back" by Baby Bash starts to play, and he stops abruptly. "Ah, Juicy, they're playing our song."

And if he wasn't perfect enough, he starts dipping his body to the beat and dances around me. Grinding his perfection on my body, lip-syncing the words, setting my soul on fire.

When it ends, I'm afraid my juice is going to drip down my leg. "Let's go, Jocko. I need you to fuck my brains out now."

"HOOYAH!"

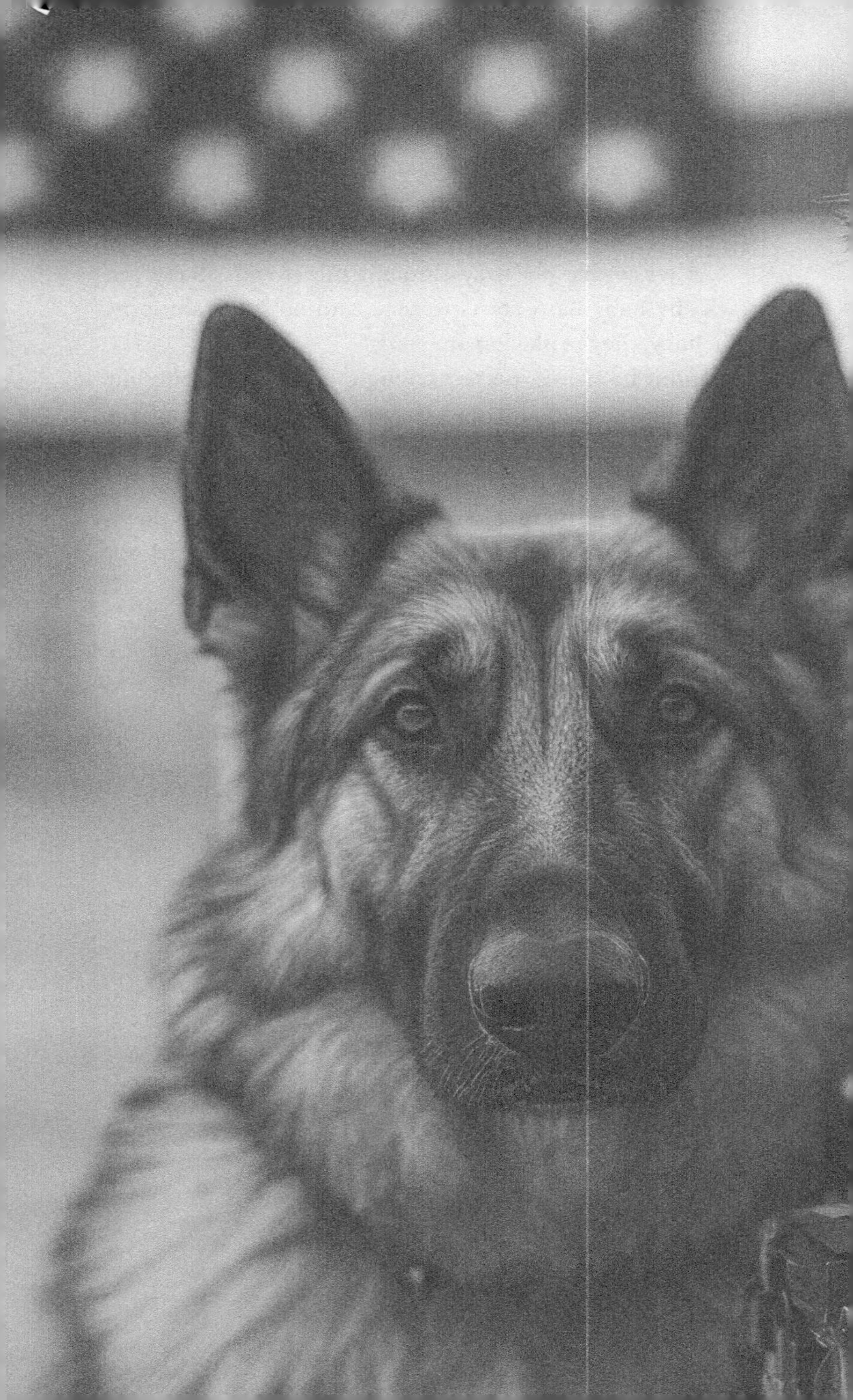

20

Jorja

We barely make it out the door before Jocko's kissing the fuck out of my mouth and making my knees so weak, I can't walk. His lips leave my mouth to nibble, trailing kisses to my ear, whispering, "Trust me" right before he lifts me off my feet. My legs wrap around his waist and my arms around his neck as he carries me around the side of the building. As he walks, he unzips his pants. In the darkness, he pins me against the brick wall then rams his erection inside as his mouth consumes my moans. To my shock, four full, hard, jolting thrusts make me cum all over him. Four more, and he cums inside me. We slump against the wall. His breath blowing my hair, tickling my neck, teasing my ear.

"My God," I mumble.

"Shh," He blows.

Then he leans back and pulls his shirt off over his head. The faintness of the light casts deep shadows along his bulging muscles as they ripple. "My god," I whisper, and I nearly cum again just looking at him.

He kisses my lips gently, barely brushing his tongue along my teeth, right before he positions his shirt between my legs and eases me down. Then he wraps his arms around me, and I drink in the essence of Jocko. His musk's intoxicating, and I feel tipsy all over again.

After a minute, he backs away, and I clean our juices off with his shirt. He takes it from me, and sticks the hem in the back of his jeans while I straighten my dress. Then we hold hands and walk to my car.

Driving back to the hotel, he reclines the seat all the way back, folds his arms over his chest, tucks his hands in so they don't slip out, and assures me, "I'm just resting my eyes."

"Umm-hmm."

At the traffic light, I marvel at how serenely beautiful his features are when his larger-than-life personality isn't playing across them. His arched brows frame heavily lashed eyes, and his nose has a slight curve, which can only mean it's been broken before. Then there are those perfect, sculpted lips that mine love to kiss. I marvel at how quickly I've fallen head over heels in love now that I've stopped fighting the attraction.

A car honks a short burst bringing me back to reality. Easing into traffic, Jocko asks, "You good, Juicy?"

"Yes, Jocko. I'm good."

He chuckles as he drifts off to sleep again, "Yes. You are. You are very good."

When I turn the blinker on at The Cottages, he doesn't

move. He's sound asleep. Making the turn at his building, the headlights shine on two men walking across the parking lot, and they stare at me as I drive by. The hair on the back of my neck rises, but I ignore it. I'm with Jocko, and I don't need to be afraid.

I turn into the empty parking spot in front of the suite. Taking the keycard from the center console, as quiet and as quickly as I can, I open the car door and step out, then push it shut, but I don't latch it. I push it just tight enough to turn the interior lights off.

Leaving the car running so Jocko doesn't wake up, I walk to the door of his suite to get Lucifer myself. The two dudes are now walking toward me down the sidewalk in front of the rooms, and they whistle, then say something vulgar. The only word I can make out is "pussy," but their tone and intent are defiant and frightening.

Ignoring them but trying to get in the room as quickly as possible before they arrive, I focus on sliding the keycard into the slot. I hit the hole, and it slips in. Right when the green lights and the latch unlocks, they swarm me—one on each side. One pushes the handle down, and the other shoves me against it. The scream that escapes is smothered by the sound of my body slamming against the door.

There's a split second of sheer terror when I realize how bad this situation is. Then I hear the car door open, and a deep, menacing voice behind us says, "Let her go, or I will fuck you up!"

A knife blade flashes as my head is jerked back by my hair, and the cold steel presses against my throat. My heartbeat pounding in my ears drowns out all ambient noises, but I hear, "Stay back, or I'll cut her," as the door swings open.

The ominous voice commands. "Stay."

"That's right. Stay back, you worthless piece of shit." The dude with the knife boasts as he pushes me inside.

I'm spun around to face the door as the other dude tries to slam it.

A massive man fills the frame, grabs him, and snatches him back out.

He squeals like a terrified coward.

The door bangs shut.

The room goes dark.

The ominous voice commands. "Guard Alert."

There is no sound.

No barking.

No snarling.

Nothing.

Until the sound of bone-crushing and blood-curdling screams deafen me.

"OU!"

I fall to the ground free.

"GET HIM OFF! GET HIM OFF!" Over and over and over.

The door swings back open and bangs hard against the wall.

The massive man fills the doorway again.

"JORJA?" Jocko searches for me.

I try to answer, but my throat's too dry.

"JORJA!" Jocko shouts over the screams as he charges into the dark room. It's a command, demanding I obey.

I manage to sputter. "I'm here."

He finds me, drops to his knees, and grabs me by the shoulders. His grip's bruising. "Are you alright?"

For just a moment longer, I'm not. Then our eyes connect. The fierceness I see scares me.

I throw my arms around him and cling to his strength. "I'm fine... now!"

His arms encircle me, pulling me tight against him, and he holds me. "I gotcha. I gotcha. It's alright."

I start to shake. "I have never been so scared in all my life."

He stares down at me and says, "Me either."

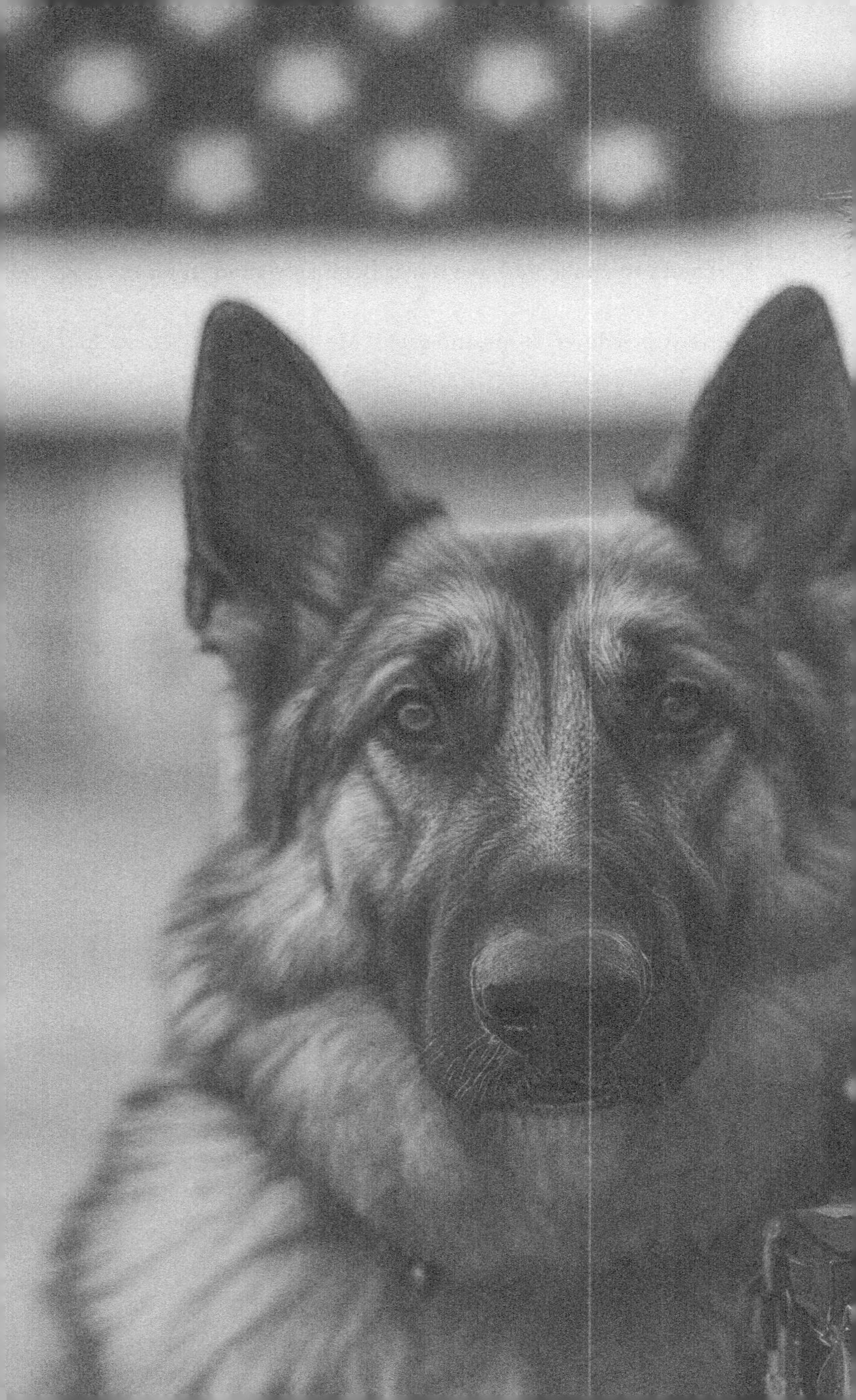

21

Jocko

The screaming stops, and she freezes. She looks up at me, terrified again, searching my eyes. "Is he dead?"

I smile. "No. He's fainted from the pain." I glance over at Lucifer, and her eyes follow.

"Are you sure? He looks dead."

"If he was dead, Luce would let go."

"Oh. That's good to know."

I pull her into my arms again and hold her. "Jorja, I'm going to grab a blanket to wrap you up in. Sit right here. Don't move."

"I'm not cold."

"You're in shock. Trust me." When I stand, she draws her legs up and cuddles herself. "Close your eyes. Don't look. I'll be right back."

She nods.

I see the knife lying on the floor and secure it. I double-check Lucifer's bite. His long canine teeth are sunk to the gums in the arm of the motherfucker who was going to rape my girl. I pat him on the back. "Good job, buddy."

He looks at me for a command to release, but I don't give it yet. Hurrying into the bedroom, I snatch a blanket off the bed and rush back to Jorja.

"Okay, Babe. Look at me."

She opens her eyes, and I offer my hand. She takes it, and I can still feel her trembling as I pull her to her feet. Wrapping the blanket around her, I shield her with my body and walk her past the blood and chaos to the car. I open the back door and tell her. "Get in and wait."

"Okay."

"Don't look."

She nods as she climbs in the backseat. I close the door and dial 911 to report what happened. Then I toss the knife on the hood and set about securing the two thugs.

The perp I knocked unconscious lays face down in a pool of his own blood. Grabbing him by his shirt and pants, I lift him up. Two teeth are left behind as I tote his unconscious body into the room. I set him down beside Lucifer.

"Luce, let go."

He blinks, shakes his head viciously one more time for good measure, spraying blood from the mangled mass, then he opens his mouth and releases the arm. It flops to the ground.

He's bloody, so I quickly check his body for injuries, but it isn't his. I praise his courage, bravery, and loyalty. "Good boy. Good job, Lucifer. You nailed the motherfucker. Excellent work, buddy." Then I tell him to, "Sit. Guard."

He sits—ears alert. Eyes focused. Tongue hanging out. Hassling from the effort. But fierce.

I roll the perp over and stare at him. I'm trained to

maintain calm on the battlefield, but this is entirely different. I'm tempted to stomp his fucking cock and bust his goddamn balls, but I hold my temper in check. The rules of engagement in the civilian world are different. Instead, I lift him by his shirt, examine his wound, making sure Lucifer didn't sever an artery. The last thing we need is for him to bleed out, then I rearrange his nose for him, plastering my fist in his face, just for good measure. The sound and the feel of his facial structure caving is satisfying.

Knowing Luce has the situation under control, I go back outside to wait for the cops.

Leaning against the wall, I breathe deep the Alabama air. Jorja opens the car door and gets out. Without saying a word, she lifts my arm and slides under it to cuddle. When the police arrive, we're still in the same position.

"The two assailants are inside. Unconscious."

He nods, and they walk to the door.

"Lucifer, come."

They stop, and the look they give me would've made me laugh under other circumstances. Luce trots out of the room, and they both take a step back, clearing out of his way.

"Oh." They smile. "Good name."

"Yeah. We each took one down."

"Let us get them secured, then we'll take your statements."

Jorja drops down to her knees and throws her arms around Lucifer, then she begins to cry. Not hard, boohoo sobs, but tears of relief. He looks up at me, and his eyes feel her pain.

When she lets him go, he licks her face making her laugh. "You're my hero, Luce. Thank you!"

He wags his tail, then lays down at our feet. She slides back under my arm to wait.

An ambulance pulls in, followed by a couple of cars that must have police scanners. Three EMT's get out. While two unload a stretcher, one walks over.

"We're good. But they're not."

He gives me a head nod and changes course. He disappears into the room, then stands in the door and waves for the stretcher.

Jorja spins around in my arms and puts her face on my chest. The feeling of holding her after being terrified that I might lose her nearly overwhelms me. I guess I'm in shock too.

But when two cops walk out with the toothless assailant in handcuffs, the lump in my throat vanishes. His face is covered in blood. His eyes are swollen shut. He has no nose that I can see, and his lips are busted. *He got off easy.*

Then the stretcher carrying the knife welding motherfucker comes out. His mauled arm lays across his chest. My fist balls up again, wanting to inflict more damage, but I force it to flex.

All three EMTs glance over at us. I give them a head nod. "Motherfuckers are lucky to be alive."

Two more cops walk out, then come over to us.

"I'm Officer Roberts. This is Officer Laramie. We can take your statements now."

I nod. "Sure."

Officer Laramie speaks to Jorja. "Ma'am, if you would walk with me over here."

She squeezes my waist, tilts her face to mine, and our eyes lock. She puckers her lips, and I give her the reassuring kiss she needs. Then she lets me go and follows him across the parking lot. I turn so that I can watch her. Her back's to me. Her arms crossed in front of her body in a defensive posture, hugging the blanket.

Her head is down. Her shoulders slumped. She speaks and nods, recalling what happened.

Officer Roberts takes a pen and a little pad out of his pocket. "What's your name?"

"Jocko Monroe."

He stops. Looks up at me. Looks down at Lucifer. Then says, "Tell me what happened." While I recount the events as they unfolded, as I was trained to do without emotion, he jots down notes for his report.

"Where's the knife?"

I point to the hood of the car.

"Does the dog have a current rabies vaccination?"

"Yes. His papers are all in order."

"Good. I don't foresee any problems. You can call tomorrow for the case number." He shakes my hand. "You may have just apprehended the perps who've been pulling off a string of armed robberies over the last few months. We won't know for sure until after the DNA tests come back, but the MO is the same."

I shake his hand and wait for Jorja to finish. When Officer Laramie closes his notepad and stuffs it in his pocket, I walk over to them. Jorja lifts my arm and cuddles up again. I shake his hand when he says, "Jocko. Nice to meet you. If you weren't already somewhat famous around here, you most certainly will be now."

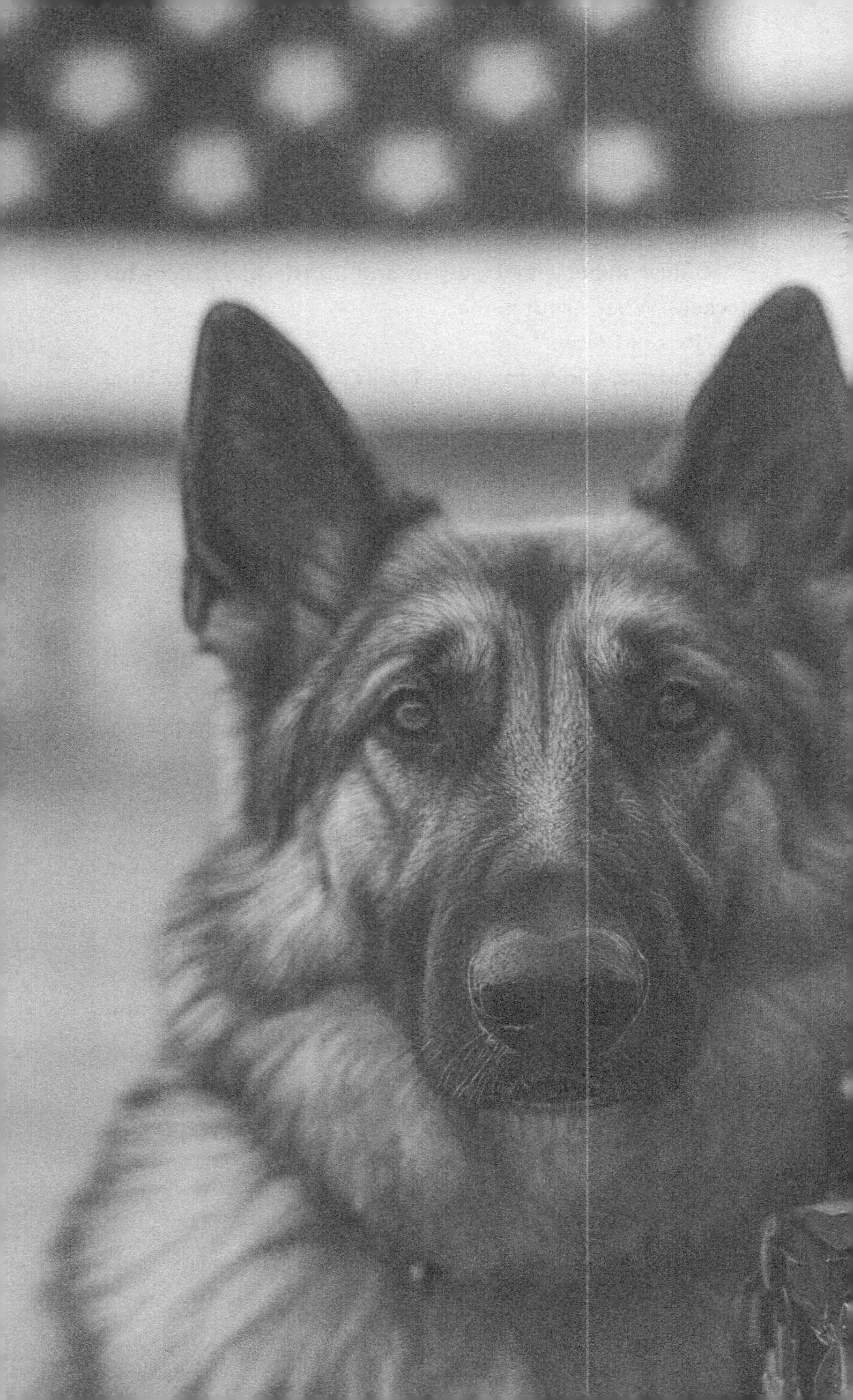

22

Jorja

"Mmm!" I stretch. "Is that coffee I smell?"

"It is." Jocko's deep voice vibrates next to my ear.

"Did *you* make coffee?"

"No. I brought it back from Donut Dilemma."

I sit up. "What time is it?"

"Almost noon."

"What?" I look around, bewildered.

He chuckles and hands me a latte cup with Donut Dilemma's logo on the side. "Your friend, Macey, wants you to call her later on when you get up."

I sit cross-legged on the bed and reach for it. "How long have you been up?"

"Since 5:00 a.m.."

"Why didn't you sleep?"

"I did, but Lucifer and I run every day at five."

"Every day?"

"Every day."

I sip my latte. "Have you eaten?"

"Yes, I went to Brother's Café for pancakes. I brought you some back."

"Mmm. I'm hungry. Thank you."

He leaves me to go into the kitchen. When I come out of the bathroom, I hear the beep of the microwave. As soon as I enter the room, Lucifer comes over and rubs his head on my legs like a cat. "Good morning, sweet boy. How's my hero?"

He wags his tail and lays at my feet when I sit down at the table. Jocko brings my plate of pancakes. He's topped them with slices of banana, sprinkled with cinnamon sugar, and drizzled with butter.

"Are you trying to spoil me?"

"Yes." He grins that sexy as fuck sideways grin. "Honey or syrup?"

"Honey."

He sets it on the table, then sits down to watch me eat.

"God, this is so good!"

"I'm an excellent cook, by the way."

"You can teach me. I'm not." I laugh. "I'm lazy, but I do love to eat."

He smiles, then says, "I received a text about an hour ago. I have to sign for my household goods."

"Oh...." I can't keep the disappointment out of my voice. "I was hoping you would be staying with me for a little while."

He grins, stands up, pushes his chair back, leans over the table, and kisses the fuck out of my mouth. "Eat your pancakes. I'll be back before you know it."

"How long will you be gone?"

"Minimum of a couple hours. It could be as many as four. The military's famous for hurry up and wait."

"Ok. I'll go to the grocery store. You eat a lot more than I do."

He laughs, opens his wallet, takes out a couple of hundred-dollar bills, and lays them on the table. "I'm pretty easy to please. I'm a meat and potatoes man. Steak, burgers, roast, chicken."

I nod. "I'll get some of each."

He sucks his lips, "Come on, Luce."

Lucifer gets up, and the new alpha males in my life walk out.

"So, did you enjoy your coffee this morning?" Macey laughs into the phone.

"As a matter of fact, I did." I laugh with her. "What time do you get off today?"

"In ten minutes. Why?"

"You won't believe what happened last night."

"What?"

"It's too much to tell over the phone. I'm going to the grocery store shopping."

"I'll meet you there."

Macey's standing at the entrance waiting on me. "So ... what happened last night? I want all the fucking details."

Walking down each aisle, I tell her everything that happened as I fill the shopping cart.

She keeps repeating two phrases. "God, the man puts some kind of food away, and you are blowing my fucking mind!"

At the checkout, as I put the items on the belt, I wrap

the story up with, "He's blown me away, Macey. Honestly. I would've never thought in a million years that any of this would be happening to me. My life's been boring, but now it's like I'm living in a story that's someone else's life."

Janice, the grocery clerk, asks, "Jorja, I apologize for being nosey, but you've been shopping here for as long as I can remember. What on earth is going on with you, girl?"

Macey jumps all into it, giving her a crash course on mine and Jocko's romance. From the beginning to the current meat order. Hearing her gush through it and watching Janice's face react gives me goosebumps. It all sounds too good to be true. Even being accosted by those horrible men just magnifies how awesome Jocko is.

As Macey and I load the bags of food into my car, she says, "I am so, so happy for you."

I give her a quick hug. "You were right all along."

She grins. "Told ya so!"

When I pull into the driveway at my house, I notice a moving truck at Mr. Finkle's.

Darn, I forgot to check with Marianne on who rented the house.

In between trips to the car to unload the food bags, I count three men carrying furniture and boxes out. Based on the jungle gym, the giant slide, and yard toys lying on the ground, I assume my new neighbor's a family. It'll be nice to hear the laughter of children again. I close the lid of the trunk and go inside to put the groceries away.

An hour later, I still haven't heard from Jocko. Knowing I need to jot down some notes now while the details are fresh to flesh out his story later, I open my laptop. But I stare at the blank scene. I should've recorded my telling Macey. I open Facebook to check-in, and the first thing I see is that I've been tagged in three pictures from last night in a post on the *Live Oak Gazette's* page.

Oh my god! This is horrible!

The first picture is of the man on the stretcher. A zoomed circle clearly shows how viciously mauled his broken arm was, complete with bone protruding and a warning that it's graphic. The second one's a close-up of the other dude walking in handcuffs without a face. The third one's Jocko, me, and Lucifer outside the hotel room. My face is buried in Jocko's chest, his arms wrapped around me, and Lucifer's lying at our feet. Two portions of that picture are zoomed to show Jocko's raw, bloody knuckles and bright red, wet patches of blood on Lucifer's black face. His eyes are glowing red from the light, and he looks like a devil dog. The caption reads, 'PTSD? Are they out of control?'

I slam the laptop closed and gulp air. *This is bad! This is very bad.*

I jump up from the table, and grab my phone to text Jocko.

> Hey. Do you know how much longer you'll be? We need to talk.

My phone rings. "Hey, Babe, missing me?"

"Yes." I smile despite my panic.

"We're wrapping up now. It shouldn't be too much longer. What's up?"

"It will keep till you get here."

"I'm not doing anything but supervising. Talk to me."

I choose my words carefully. "Something has happened."

He waits, but I'm unsure what to say over the phone. "Jorja, what has happened?"

"It's about last night, but I don't want to tell you over the phone."

"Is it important?"

"Yes."

"Is it bad?"

"I'll tell you when you get here."

The line goes dead.

I stare at it. "Did he just hang up on me?" I ask the air, then look out the window.

What I see startles me, and I step towards it, making sure I'm seeing what I think I'm seeing. "What the bloody hell?"

Jocko and Lucifer are walking over from Mr. Finkle's house!

When they walk through the front door, my mouth is no longer hanging open. It is pressed into a hard flat line.

"Sup, Juicy?"

"You're renting the house next door?" My voice sounds much more accusatory than I intended, but my heart rate is up, and I'm still shocked.

"Yeah." He stares at me.

"When were you going to tell me?" My arms cross under my boobs, and my hip cocks to the side.

"Am I in the doghouse?"

"Maybe."

"I was looking for the right time, but it didn't exactly present itself with everything that has happened between us."

I open my mouth, but he holds a finger up. "However, I did intend to tell you this morning over breakfast, but when you said you were hoping I would be staying with you for a little while longer…. Well, I decided to hold off telling you so I could sleep in your bed for that little while longer." His grin spreads to his eyes, and that cute eyebrow twitch does me in.

I roll my eyes. "You're forgiven."

He grins. "So … what happened last night that you have to tell me in person?"

I take a deep breath and sigh. "The *Live Oak Gazette* posted about the incident last night on their Facebook page. And it's not good."

He glances at my laptop. "What does it say?"

"Let me just show you."

He looks out the window, picks the laptop up off the table, takes my hand, and leads me out the door. "You can show it to me over there. I need to get back."

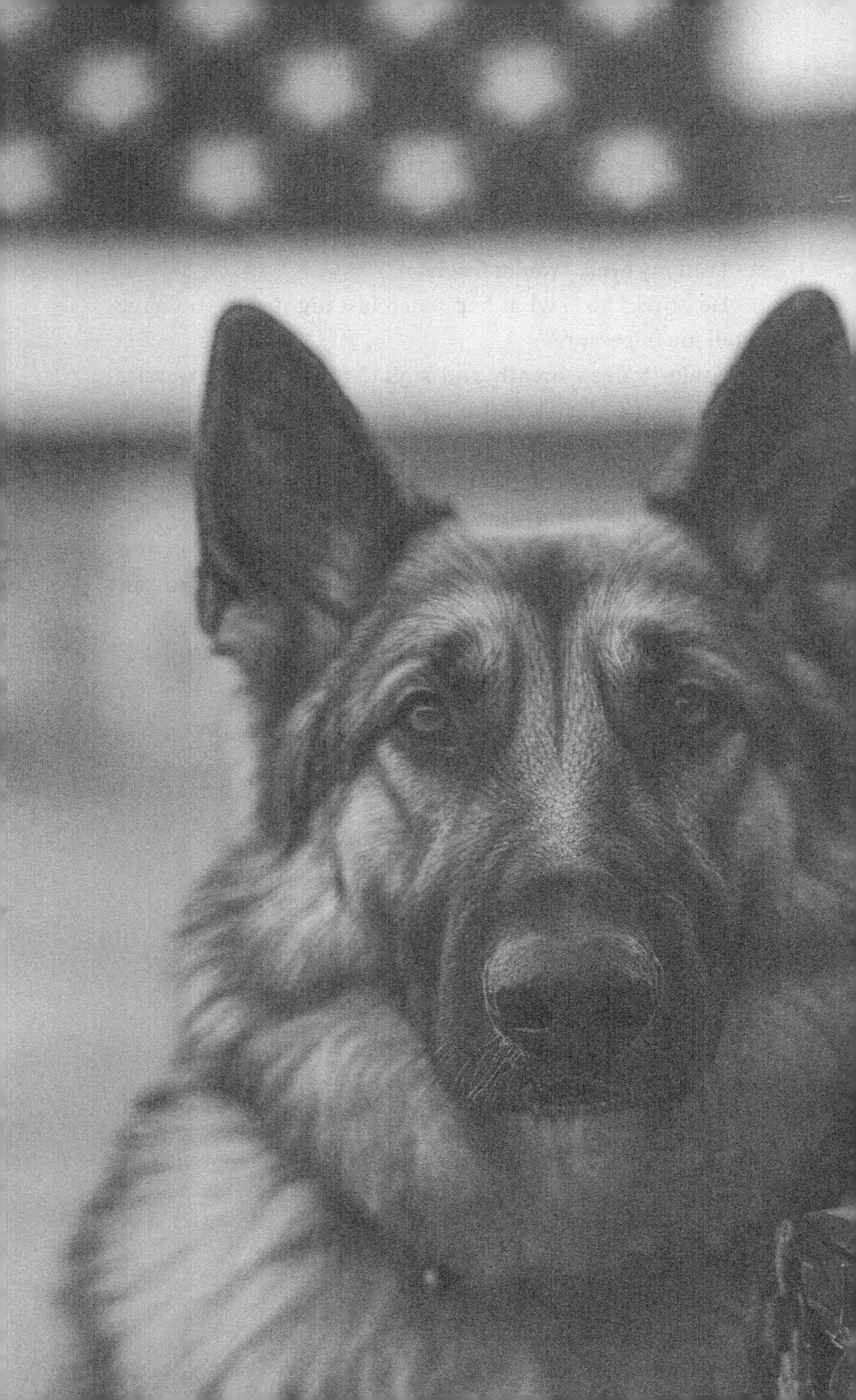

23

Jocko

"What's up with the jungle gym and the giant slide? When I came home and saw them, I assumed a family was moving in."

"They're for Lucifer's training."

"Oh." Jorja's head turns to study them as we walk by. "He's a very, very special dog, isn't he?"

The proud papa grins. "Yes. He's pretty special."

Once we're inside, I direct the men to put the boxes marked L in the second bedroom. She shows me the post on Facebook. I shrug, "So?"

"So, it's implying you two are loose cannons."

I laugh, and she frowns.

"This isn't funny, Jocko!"

"Babe, loose cannons?"

She nods.

I try to take her in my arms, but she retreats, so I stand my ground.

"I'm not worried about it, Jorja. You shouldn't either."

"But ...." Her eyebrows draw together.

"Listen, it comes with the territory of being a SEAL. People have preconceived ideas. They stereotype us. Think all sorts of batshit crazy stuff about us. That we're out-of-control killers. But the truth is SEALs are highly disciplined, trained, dedicated warriors, and so are our MPCs."

"MPCs?"

"Multi-Purpose Canines. Lucifer was a full-fledged member of the military." I stop talking. "Hang on. I'll show you. I have a box of pictures somewhere."

We walk into the second bedroom. "They're in a big box marked 'Luce Awards.'"

She bends down to spin a box around, and the view of her ass makes me smile. "Is this it?"

"Yes. That's it." I walk over, pick it up, and carry it back to the kitchen counter. Then I begin educating her on the brilliance of Lucifer. I have pictures of him in combat, doing drills, sniffing out bombs, scaling a thirty-foot fence, a series of apprehensions, and taking down enemy combatants shot from body cams. With each one, I share with her the story behind it.

"Wow!" She stares at all the pictures. "These are awe-inspiring."

"Yeah. Like I said, he's pretty special."

The last one is of him standing proud at his retirement ceremony with his medal pinned on his vest and his award hanging on a ribbon around his neck. I'm kneeling next to him, showing his certificate of retirement.

"He isn't a loose cannon. He is never out of control."

Her brows draw together. "But people will be afraid of him after that post."

I shrug. "It doesn't matter. We don't care."

"I know, but I care."

"That's because you're sweet." I put a wild, stray hair behind her ear. "But I've already thought of needing to introduce Luce to Live Oak correctly. I spoke to Emmy, and we're going to do a K9 skills demonstration at the Fourth of July event. Once people see how he works, they'll stop worrying about him. Besides, I know this talented writer at *Southern Family* that's going to do a killer feature spread on us that will set the record straight."

She takes a deep breath. "I'll do you proud. I promise."

"I know you will, Babe."

Jorja

Within the hour, the movers have gone. Jocko finds a box marked Lucifer's inside toys and takes it with us back to my house.

They sit on the floor in the living room, and I snap pictures of them playing as if it's Christmas, and all the chew toys inside are new. It's the cutest thing ever. Watching them roll around on the floor together. Playing tug of war and grab-ass.

When they have both had enough, Lucifer goes into his crate. "He likes his crate, doesn't he?"

Jocko climbs up on the couch with me. "It's his safe zone."

"Oh."

Lucifer closes his eyes and falls asleep. Jocko puts his head in my lap and says, "Tomorrow, we'll put together his jungle gym."

"I'm not very handy when it comes to tools."

He laughs. "Your training will begin in earnest then."

I trace my finger down the side of his face, enjoying the way my fingertips tingle when I touch him.

"Mmm, that feels good." He closes his eyes.

He is so incredibly handsome. I run my fingers through his hair, then massage his temples. His breathing slows, and his chest rises and falls in a steady rhythm.

I grin. He's sleeping again. I lean my head back and close my eyes too.

I wake to the smell of something delicious and discover Jocko in the kitchen cooking. Lucifer is in his crate on his back, all four paws in the air, looking at me.

When I walk into the kitchen, I look around. My kitchen doesn't look the same. It's organized.

Jocko stops chopping. "I hope you like tacos."

"I love tacos!" I walk over for a kiss, and he gives me a quick peck.

"Sit down. I'll serve you."

I run my fingers through my hair and stare up at him. "Are you sure I'm not dreaming?"

He grins, and gives me another quick peck. "I tell you what, let's agree to never wake up."

We stare at each other for what feels like forever, finally communicating silently on the same level.

"Deal."

"Beer?"

"Yes, please."

Over the next week, our days develop a routine.

At 4:45 a.m., we rise. By 5:00 a.m., Jocko and Lucifer hit the pavement for their daily five-mile run while I write.

Three times a week, they take Ms. Jenkins' dog Tipper with them.

When they return, we shower, cook breakfast, eat, clean up, then work on Lucifer's playground together.

In the afternoons, Jocko and Lucifer train while I cheer, clap, laugh and gasp in amazement at all the things Lucifer can do. My favorite by far isn't in the physical agility he has, although that alone is impressive as hell, but rather the intelligence and focus he shows when he balances a glass of water on the bridge of his nose and walks across the yard. His concentration is stunning. He's nimble, agile, dexterous, and graceful, all at the same time.

Again and again, I'm blown away by the level of love, commitment, and loyalty they have for each other. But more than that, I admire the integrity, honor, and discipline that make up Jocko's character and permeate everything he does. Always front and center, he instills these qualities to Lance on the three days a week that Lance comes after school to learn how to be a dog handler.

Our evenings are spent in each others' arms, cuddling on the couch watching television or reading, or christening a different room depending on where we are when the mood moves us. I learn that sex on the dryer is one of my favorite ways to do laundry.

At night, when the world is still, I stay awake just to

watch him sleep. The peaceful calm of his features assures me that good always wins and that true love is worth fighting for. Then I close my eyes and cuddle to stay warm because he's a cover hog.

Every day, somewhere during my waking hours, I realize that if I hadn't already fallen in love with him, that at that moment in time, I would. Jocko Monroe is my hero.

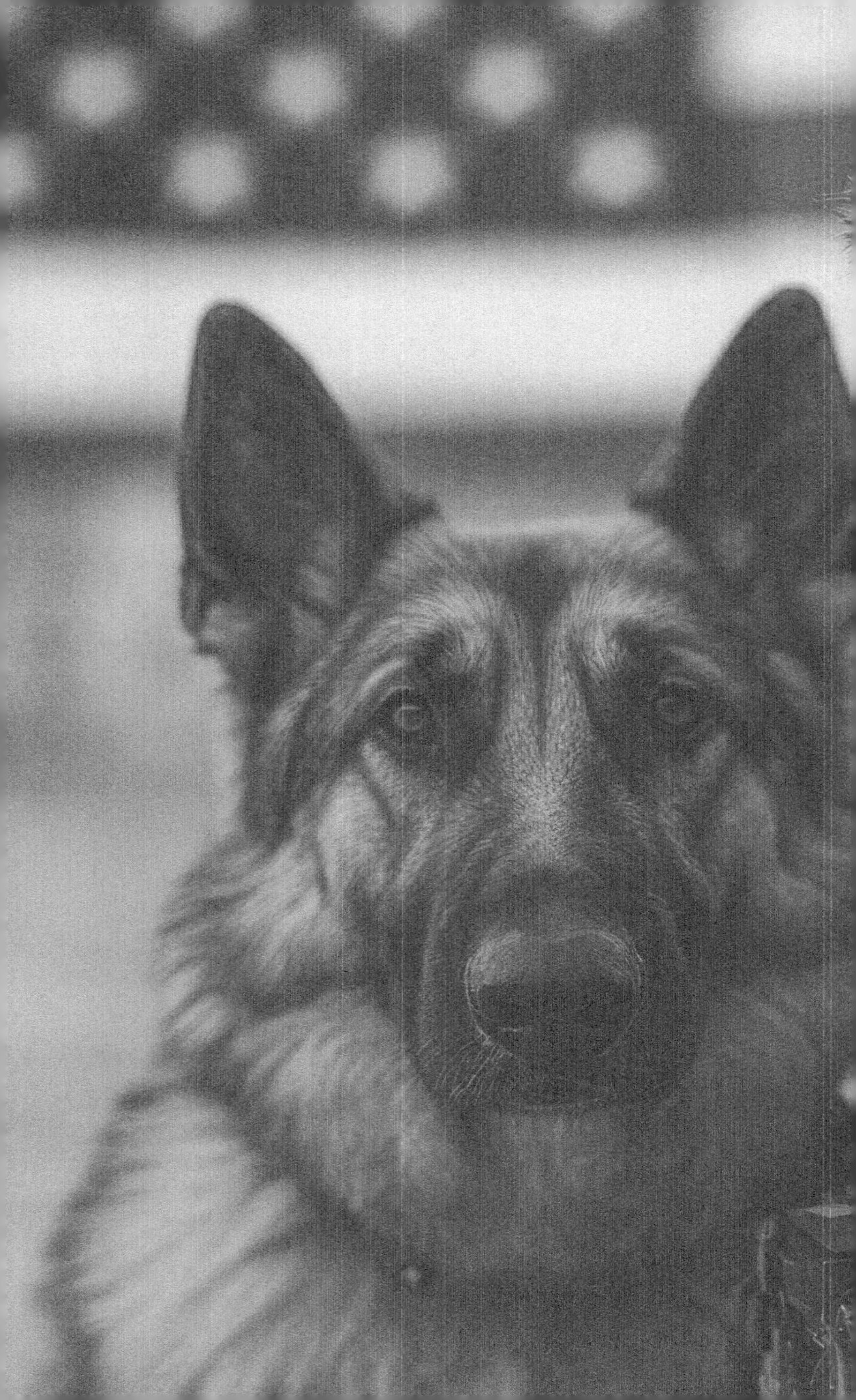

24

Jocko

The pilot cues the mic. "Jocko, we are thirty seconds to target."

I give him a thumbs-up, pick Lucifer up, secure his harness, give him a quick 'good boy' pat, then step into the hole.

The view is spectacular.

Blue skies. No clouds. A perfect day.

"Five, four, three, two, one, JUMP!"

Free-falling is an exhilarating feeling nearly as good as sex. Nearly.

I check Lucifer. He's good.

I check my G-shock watch.

Pull the parachute in five, four, three, two, one.

Ripcord pulled.

Review the landing sequence.

Recheck my G-shock.

Pop the smoke canisters in five, four, three, two, one. Bingo.

Spiral my way down to the white X marking the landing zone, then alter the course of my life forever.

Jorja

He is just a speck in the sky.

A tiny dot.

The crowd of people around me has no idea he's there. But I know. My heart is well aware that the man who holds it dear is free-falling at God knows how many miles per hour, hurtling through the air toward the ground.

My heart is racing. My breath is shallow. My hands are sweaty. My throat is dry.

His parachute opens, and a sigh of relief exits my body.

Darcy, the photographer, leans over and says, "I'm getting some great shots."

I nod. "Thanks."

Demi walks up. "We are all set. This is going to be epic."

I nod again. My eyes glued to the red, white, and blue parachute spiraling down towards us.

Emmy, standing about twenty feet off the white X marking the landing zone, taps the microphone and directs the crowd to look up.

Gasps, and cheers, and clapping erupt when Jocko pops the smoke canisters.

My heart swells with pride. He is such a good man.

Emmy begins the introductions letting the crowd know who he is.

"Ladies and gentlemen, Wings Away is proud to announce the arrival of Jocko Monroe and his K9, Lucifer. These two special operators served honorably as Navy SEALs and have recently retired in Live Oak. Both are decorated war heroes and deserve a round of applause."

The crowd claps enthusiastically. Someone begins to chant, "USA, USA, USA," and the mantra grows.

Emmy begins talking again, and they quiet down to listen.

She explains that as soon as they land, Lucifer will be doing a K9 skills demonstration on the obstacle course set up on the field.

"Then the first annual contest for Live Oak's Top Dog will begin. The dog crowned will be featured in *Southern Family Magazine* and receive a $500 cash prize. But, right now, let's enjoy the show."

The crowd cheers, but I barely hear them. My heart has jumped back in my throat. Jocko and Luce are descending rapidly, and the expression 'coming in hot' gets stuck in my head. I know I shouldn't worry, Jocko has done this hundreds of times, but I have not.

Each time I witness something he does that to me is extraordinary, he always laughs it off with, "It's no big deal, Babe."

But it is. It is a very big deal. He is a very big deal.

I marvel now at the difference in his attitude from the cocky, arrogant ass in high school to this confident yet unpretentious man. Knowing he made the right choice to become a SEAL rather than a professional baseball player.

Circling overhead, his gorgeous gloriousness is on full display. I can see his bright white teeth smiling from here.

He is enjoying himself immensely, and that makes me happy.

Nearing the landing, he flares the chute, and his speed adjusts dramatically. He flares it again and lands light as a feather on his feet. The crowd cheers as he releases the fabric. Leroy and a couple of employees from Wings Away rush up to gather it and take it out of the way.

Emmy, Lance, and I walk up to them as he releases Lucifer from his harness.

Luce lands on his feet like a cat. His eyes and ears focused on Jocko, waiting for his instructions.

Emmy congratulates Jocko on a successful jump, then sticks the microphone under his nose. He encourages anyone interested in learning to skydive to get in touch with Wings Away.

"Thank you for the endorsement. Wings Away appreciates it. While you were on your way down, I explained to the crowd that Lucifer was going to give us a demonstration of his K9 skills." She sticks the microphone back under his nose.

He nods and explains that what they are going to witness Lucifer do, is what makes him a valuable asset to Special Operations. That MPC K9's, like Lucifer, are full-fledged members of the military, then he looks at Lance, who takes Lucifer's leash and hooks him up. "Lance Monroe is going to assist me today with the demonstration, but first, I would like to take a moment to ...."

He turns his laser-like focus on me.

My heart stops instantly.

His eyes lock on mine, and the sheer intensity in his stare takes my breath away.

The world stops spinning as he walks over, and I know

a hush has fallen over the crowd, but all I'm aware of is the magnificence that is Jocko.

When he is standing directly in front of me, towering down, he asks, "Jorja? Do you know what's about to happen?"

He nods at me. "That's right. I'm going to brazenly kiss you again. Do you know why?"

He rakes his eyes over my body, and every nerve comes alive.

"Because I really, really, want to taste your sweetness. But first, I'm going to ask you something, and then I'm going to kiss the fuck out of your mouth, and you are going to kiss the fuck out of mine. Because deep down inside, you are ready for me to rock your fucking world forever."

I start to shake.

"So, get ready. This is me, asking you to be my wife."

He drops to one knee. "Juicy," he opens a little black ring box, "Will you marry me?"

An explosion of happiness bursts forth as tears of joy, mixed with laughter, and 'yeses' upon 'yeses' erupt from within. I fling myself into his arms as he stands, and he catches me easily, then he kisses the ever-loving fuckity fuck out of my mouth.

I can barely make out the sound of cheers and Emmy's congratulations over the blood thundering in my ears. I'm vaguely aware that Lance has taken Lucifer away as Jocko rocks my world with his earth-shattering kiss. I have no idea how long we indulge ourselves, but it's long enough that the crowd's attention has moved on.

When Jocko lets me down, he places a sweet, tender kiss on my forehead, then grins at me with that little twitch of his eyebrow that is so damn cute. He holds the ring out, and I present my fingers. He slides it on and tells me. "This was my mom's."

My heart melts, knowing that not only does Jocko want to be my husband, but he wants to be the father of my children. I jump into his arms again, and he twirls us around.

We walk hand in hand over to watch Lance putting Lucifer through his training. Luce is up on top of the parallel bars, working his way across. Each foot moves independently of the other. His exceptionalism on full display. Demonstrating to everyone he shouldn't be feared.

He is a hero too.

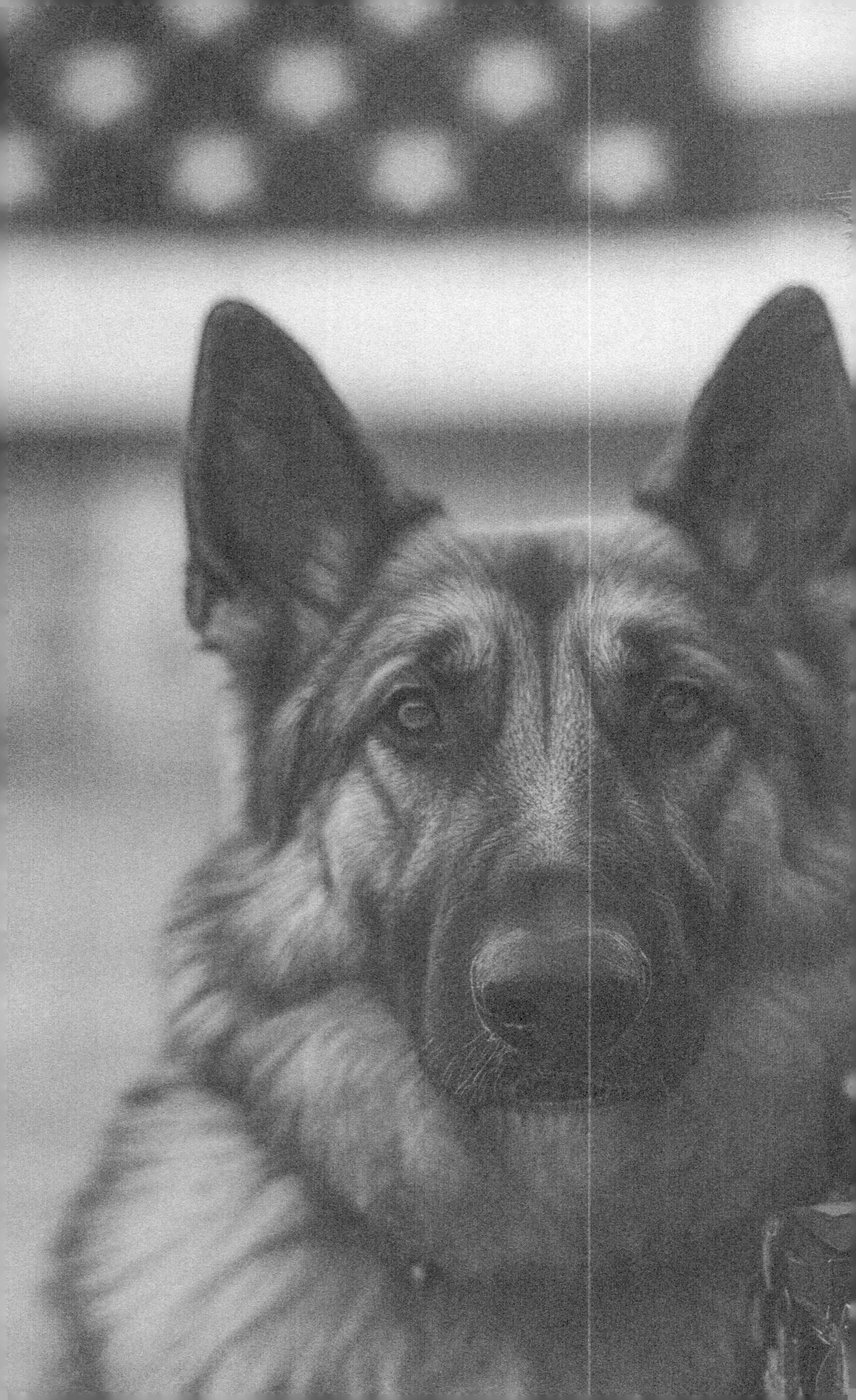

25

Four months later.

Jocko

Jorja wanted me to wear my dress whites with all my medals instead of a tuxedo. But the look on my family's faces when I stepped out wearing it, showed their shock and awe. Especially Lance's face. His eyes bugged out, and his jaw dropped. The area where they are pinned on my left chest is completely covered.

I smirk at them. "I'm the same man I was ten minutes ago."

Bradley shakes his head. "Yeah, but ten minutes ago, we didn't know what a true hero you obviously are. Damn, man. That's an impressive patch of ribbons."

Greg says, "Gotta have the story behind 'em when you two get back from your honeymoon."

I nod and chuckle. "You do know my missions were classified."

"Yeah, but you gotta give us something."

Penny, the wedding planner, arrives and gathers us all together for our trip to the church. She takes one look at me and whistles, "Impressive!"

Then she informs us Jorja and the bridal party are already onsite. As soon as we arrive, I'm to take my place in the holding chamber with the priest, and the groomsmen are to escort the guests to their seats. Then at two minutes till 6 p.m. sharp, "Just like we rehearsed last night. Any questions?"

―――

Jorja

―――

"Stop fidgeting," Sandy tells me. "You'll mess up your hair."

I stand in the vestibule of the church, waiting for Uncle John to walk me down the aisle. "I'm nervous," I tell her.

She smiles, "Nonsense, you're excited."

I laugh with her. "Okay. I'm so excited it feels like nerves."

She walks around me with her eye for detail and says, "You are perfection right now, Jorja. And when Jocko sees you.... Well, he's going to have a hard time keeping his emotions in check."

I smile at her. "It'll crush his image."

She laughs, "Yeah, but a little humility will go a long way to solidify his humanity."

I laugh. "I don't know. I'm not sure I want him to be less cocky. Now that I understand him, his badass persona is such a turn-on."

She laughs, "Trust me when I tell you this. Long term, *you* need to remember your perfection at this moment forever. There will be times in the future when you will be at your absolute worse, and you can draw on this moment for assurance that he knows how beautiful you are and despite the current circumstances, you'll see the same look in his eyes then as now, and understand the depth of love he has for you." She eyes my small protruding belly.

I laugh, "I hear you."

A light rap on the door draws her around my gown to face me. She reaches for my hands. "Jorja Jones, I can't wait to call you a Monroe."

The door cracks, and Macey pokes her head inside. "Sandy, you need to line up. I got her."

Sandy gives my hands one last squeeze, then she walks out. Macey takes her place in the small room with me, but she's not calm, cool, or collected. She's a nervous mess and paces back and forth.

"Jorja, are you sure?"

I roll my eyes. "Are you serious right now?"

She giggles apprehensively. "Yes, and no."

I laugh. "Yes, I'm positive!"

"Good, because I need you to be."

"I have no doubts about marrying Jocko, Macey."

She sighs. "I don't either. I don't know what's wrong with me."

There is another light knock on the door, and Macey

rushes to it. She opens it, and Uncle John smiles at her. "Macey...."

"Oh, gosh! It's time." She looks back at me. "You look beautiful, boo!"

"You do too. Now, go."

She takes a deep breath and passes Uncle John. He watches her leave, then looks in. "You ready, Jorja?"

"Yes, sir. I'm ready."

"Then let's get you married into the family."

Jocko

The guests rise as the traditional wedding march begins. I stand facing the aisle, waiting for my girl to appear. My heart is light, happy, thrilled, and nervous, all at the same time. I swallow the emotions building. My training kicking in.

Then I see the top of Uncle John's head, and everything I thought I had control of flies away. Jorja comes into view, and the world stops revolving. She looks like an angel. Her face is radiant with a flush of color. *Nerves,* I smile. Her hair is braided and piled on top of her head. Interlaced are little white daisies. Her elegant carriage and long neck are highlighted by her sleeveless gown. The bouquet of flowers clutched in her hand shake with her excitement.

The joy inside my soul is incomprehensible, and when she lifts her eyes and meet mine, tears leak out.

Two months later.

Jocko

Sitting at the table watching my wife about to receive her award for the article she wrote on Heroes Among Us about Lucifer and me, I look over at Greg. He is wearing the same look on his face watching Sandy preparing to give her the award.

Sandy holds the plaque, steps up to the microphone, and addresses the crowd. "On behalf of *Southern Family Magazine* and Thompson Publishing House, it is my great honor to award Jorja Monroe the First Annual Thompson Publishing House Best Writers Award for her article titled "Rules of Engagement, Coming Home for Her" on Heroes Among Us, featuring Jocko Monroe and his K9 Lucifer." She points to us, and the spotlight finds us.

I give a small wave of acknowledgment that Luce, who is lying at my feet, and I were the subjects of the article.

"I would also like to take this moment to congratulate Jorja on becoming a *Wall Street Journal, New York Times,* and *USA Today* Bestselling Author for her subsequent book entitled *Rules of Engagement, Making Relationships Work.*"

She turns to Jorja and says, "Congratulations on both." Then she hands her the plaque and backs away from the spotlight.

Jorja looks down at the award for a moment, then she steps up to the microphone and graciously but humbly accepts the accolades from her peers for her article.

When I read it, I was impressed by her ability to tell our tale in the manner that she did. She presented our story from the eyes of a woman who came to know and love her hero and who now understands why I did what I did and do what I do.

I was touched, and after reading it, I knew I would never have to worry about any miscommunication with Jorja ever again. She's actually a great communicator, which is why she's a journalist and a bestselling author.

She clears her throat, and I tune out my thoughts and tune in to her voice.

"Jocko Monroe is the epitome of a hero. He served his country with distinction as a special operator, a Navy SEAL. The words love, devotion, honor, trust, and respect are the keystones of his character. They are the words at the very core of who Jocko Monroe is, and they are what make him a hero.

Every day he proves it to me in one way or another. Some days it's the big ways, like rescuing a lost man in the woods or saving me from two armed attackers.

But most days, it's the little things, like kissing me goodbye. Every. Single. Time... he leaves me for longer than thirty minutes."

She smiles as she looks at me, and I remember the conversation all too well. We didn't see eye to eye on that point. I thought it wasn't necessary. But she straightened my ass out, and she explains it to the audience too.

"If he doesn't return to me, I want to be assured that the last thing I did was kiss him, and the last words I heard would be our 'I love you's.'

You see, it's important to me because the first time he left me, he kissed me, but he didn't say 'I love you', and we spent six long years not knowing that we were on the same page. Communication is key.

Now, even though we know that we love each other and it really isn't necessary to say every day, he does it for me because it is one of my 'Rules of Engagement.'

He isn't just *a* hero. He is *my* hero."

The crowd collectively chuckles.

She waits until she has their attention again. "I encourage each of you to look around at the men and women who are in your life with a new appreciation for the work they unselfishly do on behalf of the community. Our collective heroes among us."

She pauses, letting the emphasis build on her next words. "But to also look around at the men and women who are a part of your personal life. Your husbands, wives, partners, and see them for what they are to you. They are the ones who put in the time on *your* behalf in *your* relationships. It's the giving of these heroes among us that's done on our behalf, not necessarily agreeing or understanding of it, but the doing of it out of a mutual love, devotion, honor, trust, and respect. The keystones of what makes a relationship the best it can be."

"Establish your own Rules of Engagement, and let Rule Number One be making sure your Hero Among Us knows that... Every. Single. Day... they are not only loved but appreciated."

The room stands and applauds.

THREE MONTHS LATER.
FRIDAY AT 5:35 A.M.

Jorja

"Okay! That just happened." I stare at the puddle of clear liquid between my feet. "That is juicy on a whole other level!"

I text Sandy first.

> Morning, Boss Lady. I won't be coming to work. My water just broke. Since things are going to happen fast now, I'm texting Lance the details for Luce.

> I apologize if he reads this before you do and wakes you before six.

I text Lance next.

> Good morning, Sir Lance-a-lot. Guess what? Today is baby day!

> Luce's food is labeled in the fridge. Feed him around 6. He can have 2 treats during the day, but no more. (He is getting fat.) There are balloons in the garage if you want to blow some up and play. I have his toys in his overnight bag. Thank you again for looking out for our boy! It means the world to us knowing he is being spoiled rotten while we are gone.

Then I text Jocko.

Coming Home for Her

> Head on back, Baby Daddy. It's time for our girl to join us.

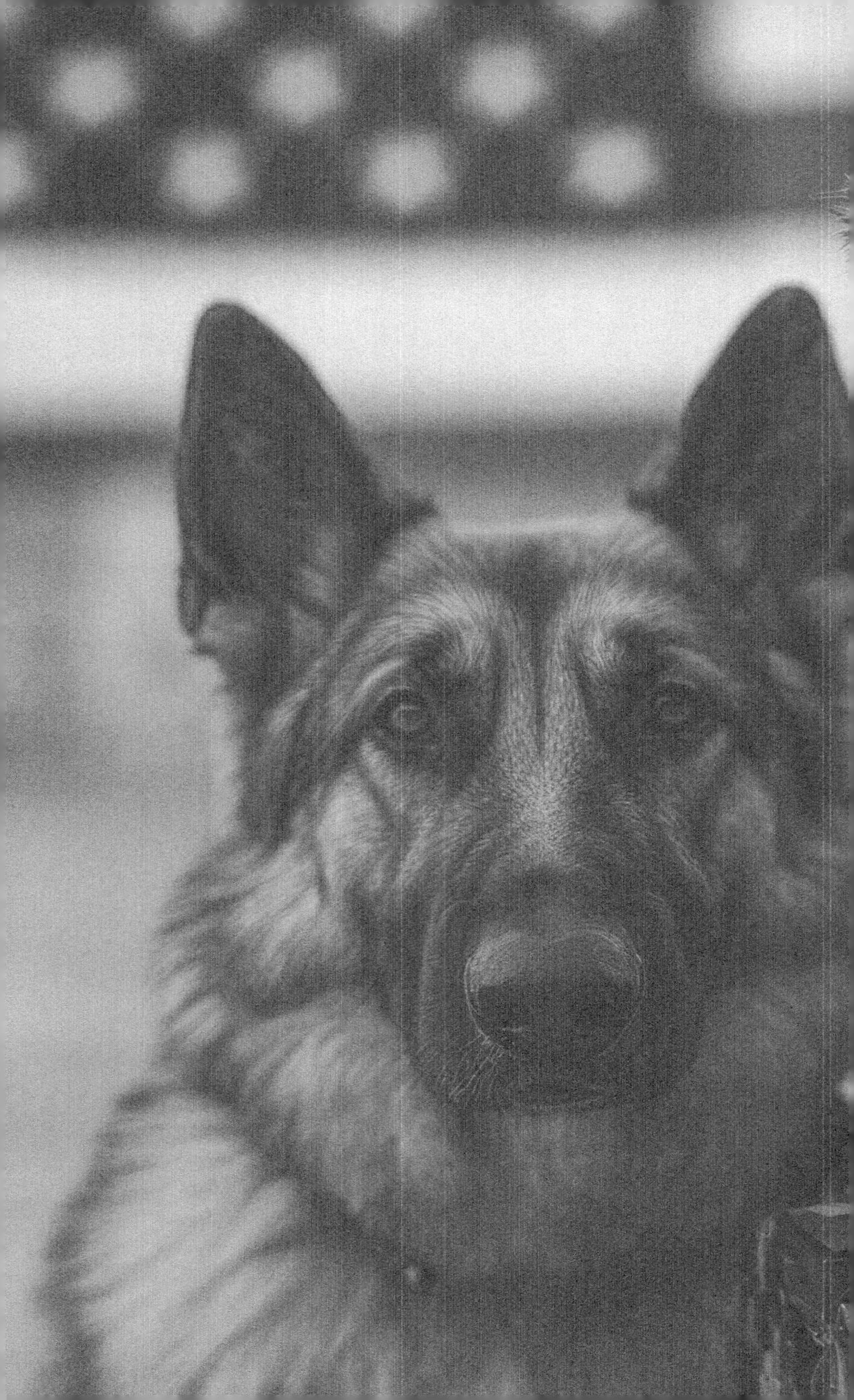

Epilogue

FIVE YEARS LATER...

Jorja

"Hush, Little Baby, hmmm, hmmm, hmmm."

...

...

I smile, content, listening to Jocko's deep voice singing softly to Jordyn, then I close my eyes, drifting back to sleep. "He's such a good daddy."

...

...

"Mommy.... Mommy.... Can I sleep with you and Daddy?"

I open my eyes and look into the sweet little face of Jade

Ann with her pure green eyes like Jocko's. They are big as saucers as she leans against the bed, putting her face inches from mine.

I pat the mattress, and she climbs up. "Did you have a bad dream?"

"No," She tells me as she crawls over me to get to her daddy. "I just want to snuggle." She coos as she wiggles between us.

"Hmm." I close my eyes again.

...

...

The mattress sags from the weight of two paws pressing down. Then a nose roots around, searching for my arm under the covers. I open one eye and peer at our boy. I push my arm out from under the covers, and his cold nose pokes it. "Luce, did you have a bad dream?"

He pokes it again.

"Do you want to snuggle too?"

He pokes it again.

"Ah, you need to go outside?"

He flops his ears, then waits for movement.

The soft sounds of peaceful sleep next to me assure me I'm the only one who will assist him. I lift my head, and his alert eyes meet my drossy ones.

When I push the covers off, he heads out of the room but waits outside the bedroom door for me. With my first step, he turns, and I follow him down the hall to the back door.

Passing the kitchen, I glance at the clock. It's midnight. At the door, I put my hands on my hips and ask him, "Did Jade Ann slip you goodies under the table again?"

He doesn't answer, of course. But the urgency in his

eyes assures me she did. As soon as I open the backdoor, he slips through the crack and vanishes. Walking out onto the porch, I lean against the handrail and look up at the stars. My eyes adjust to the moonlight, and I watch him lap the perimeter, checking that we are safe before he jumps over the fence to do his business in the woods.

In no time, he's back, and we go inside. When I shut the door and lock it, he waits for my kiss on his head before he trots over to his bed in the living room. When I pass my baby girl's room, I peek in on her. Jordyn is sleeping peacefully in her crib, so I go back to bed.

When I gently lift the covers to slide back under, Jocko's hand reaches for me. He may be asleep, but I swear his ears hear everything. Always aware of where his family is. With a gentle squeeze of acknowledgment that we're safe, I lean over and give him a kiss.

His steady even breathing makes me smile. He's already deep asleep before I can settle back in.

I sigh. *Life is good.*

Jocko

Jade Ann giggles, and I shush her as I lift her from the bed, then tiptoe out with her waving to Jorja. As I shift her on my hip, closing the door, my wife's beautiful face peeks out of her tangled mop of bed hair to blow me a kiss. I lift my chin, acknowledging her love with a nod, and she slips back under the covers to sleep.

Jorja was forced to loosen her Rules of Engagement with the arrival of Jade Ann, and I'm no longer required to kiss her before going on my morning run. She needs to sleep when she can, but she sleeps with one eye open, always aware of where her family is.

Jade Ann and I peek in on Jordyn; she's standing in the crib playing fetch with Luce. She tosses over a stuffed animal, and it sails across the room. He picks it up and puts it back in.

Hmm. She's got a good arm. She's going to be my ballplayer.

I look at Jade Ann, and she nods, so I swing the door open, and we walk in.

Jordyn's sweet smile, which looks exactly like Jorja's, greets us as she leans on the railing and reaches up.

Luce sits, wagging his tail, with a stuffed unicorn in his mouth. Jade Ann leans down to him, pats his head, and tells him as she takes it from him. "Thanks for babysitting, Luce. You're a good boy."

Jordyn coos from the crib, excited, marching in place.

Jade Ann pulls herself upright on my hip and tells me as we walk over to Jordyn. "What would we do without him?"

I laugh at her and kiss the top of her head. "I don't know. I honestly don't know."

At the crib, Jade Ann tosses the Unicorn in, then leans down to kiss the top of Jordyn's head, "Morning, Sissy, do you want to go running with me and daddy?"

Jordyn grunts, then says, "Da da."

Jade Ann goes stiff, and she looks at me with her big green eyes. "Daddy! She said, 'Da da!'"

I laugh again as I pick up my other baby girl, accepting her messy hugs and kisses. "So, she did."

Walking over to the changing table, I set Jade Ann in the

chair next to it and lay Jordyn down. Jade Ann blabs to her while we work as a team to put a dry diaper on her and a clean onesie.

Jade Ann is a natural leader. She steps up and helps whenever she can and understands more than she can physically do. Jorja calls her, 'Little Miss Bossy Britches.'

When I pick them both back up in my arms, Luce leads the way to the kitchen. I set Jade Ann down, and she follows Luce into the laundry room to dress while I retrieve Jordyn's morning bottle.

Once we are all set, we hit the road. Luce leads the way, followed by Jordyn in our baby jogging stroller, me pushing it, and Jade Ann strapped on my back in our baby hikers backpack.

The sky is clear this morning, and the moon has already set. The stars twinkle bright overhead. We run our daily route with only the sound of my breath and my feet hitting the road. The hypnotic rhythm always puts the girls back to sleep.

As the sun begins to rise, Jade Ann wakes first. She doesn't say anything. I just feel her little arms hug me.

Life is good.

When we turn onto Magnolia Street, heading back home, Mr. Davis, coffee cup in hand, opening his car door, throws his hand up. "Good morning, Jocko. You and your girls have a good day."

I wave to him, and although I can't see her, I know Jade Ann is too.

Back at the house, Jorja greets up at the door. She has showered and is dressed. She scoops Jordyn up as I gently set Jade Ann down and unstrap her.

"Did you all have a good run this morning? Are you

ready to eat some breakfast?" She asks them, then she kisses me before she takes Jade Ann's hand. "I thought we would ride with you to the airport."

I grin at her. "So that's why you're dressed with your hair and makeup on before nine a.m."

She swats me, then turns to take our girls inside, explaining that Daddy has a new client coming into town today that is a celebrity, and they will be going with me to get her and her dog from the airport.

Jade Ann immediately begins asking questions, and I chuckle. "She's going to be an investigative reporter, you know."

Jorja laughs, nodding, and she begins answering Jade Ann as they walk into the house. "Her name is Siri Moore, and her dog's name is Angel. She's a famous Los Vegas entertainer. Daddy and Lucifer are going to train her and Angel."

Jade Ann and Jordyn both look back at Luce and me watching them.

Jade Ann asks, "Daddy and Luce are going to teach them how to be heroes?"

Jorja stops and looks back at us too. Her expression is everything, and when our eyes connect, she says, "Yes, he is."

Ah! My world is complete.

Thank you for reading
COMING HOME FOR HER
I hope you loved Jocko, Jorja, and Luce and will choose to leave a review for others.

Coming Home for Her

Want more Jocko and Lucifer?
You'll find them in a spinoff series by Jessika's pen name, Stingray23, in
No Love Left Behind

Want to Read Jessika's newest, sexiest, and most talked about bestsellers?

Learn more at

JessikaKlide.com/bookstore

Jessika Klide

Jessika Klide brings readers the perfect blend of heat, humor, and heart.
Help spread the word about her books by leaving a review on your favorite book site.
Thank you!

JOIN JESSIKA'S VIP READER'S LIST
https://jessikaklide.com/

Newsletters not your thing?
No worries.
— CONNECT ON SOCIAL MEDIA —
Goodreads: https://tinyurl.com/JKonGR

- tiktok.com/@authorjessikaklide
- instagram.com/jessikaklideauthor
- facebook.com/JessikaKlideRomance
- bookbub.com/authors/jessika-klide
- x.com/JessikaKlide